THREE GIRLS

KATIE CLAPHAM

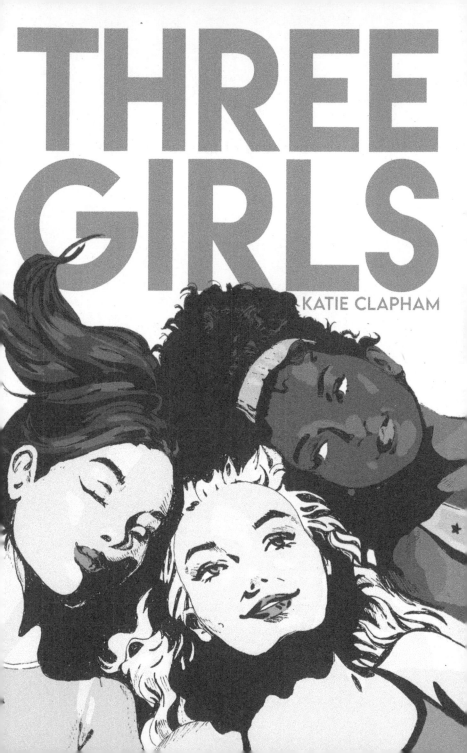

THREE GIRLS

KATIE CLAPHAM

For/Because of Louise Lamont

Three Girls is a uclanpublishing book

First published in Great Britain in 2022 by
uclanpublishing
University of Central Lancashire
Preston, PR1 2HE, UK

First published in the UK 2022

Text copyright © Katie Clapham 2022
Cover artwork © Erin Jones 2022

978-1-912979-80-6

1 3 5 7 9 10 8 6 4 2

Set in 11.5/18pt Kingfisher by Amy Cooper

A CIP catalogue record for this book is available from the British Library.

Printed and bound in Great Britain by Clays Ltd, Elcograf S.p.A.

ALICE

Listen to this and then tell me it isn't outrageous.

I was mooching up the hill, minding my own and, OK let's be real, I *did* look particularly nice due to the photo thing at school. I might have been up at stupid a.m. to fix my hair and I was wearing an actual ironed shirt, a fitted one because Mum says they look smarter than the baggy ones. I had new tights on. Like, brand new. Smart and studious is what I was going for because that's the photo I've been chosen to be in with the other academic over-achievers. It's one of those privileges that makes you momentarily wish you were a bit less brilliant.

Anyway, I looked good and it was warm-ish so I tucked my blazer through my bag strap and I guess it got caught on my skirt and hiked it up at the back a bit because the next thing I knew a car was slowing down right next to me and this . . . face hangs out the window and smiles at me in this way that makes me realise I've never really known what 'leering' was, but it was definitely happening and it was definitely disgusting. His eyes rolled over my body and he grinned as if we were sharing a joke. As if I knew what he was thinking and maybe I was thinking it too. As if that were even vaguely possible, in this actual real life where I am a fifteen-year-old girl going to school and he is a grown man behaving incredibly inappropriately!

And then he said, no word of a lie, "Hit me, Britney, one more time!"

I stopped in my tracks, because this is nuts, right? And I said, "What?!!?"

And he said it again! But this time he thrust his chest out and made this awful expression with some strange groaning noise and I was really not sure what was going on, until he clarified exactly.

"No school boy can handle all of *that*." And that's when I turned and ran.

LENA

The photographer makes us do it again and again. "Don't run so fast!" he says, like anyone is going to run slow on purpose so he gets a better shot. "Can you bunch together, girls, maybe?" he suggests. "Arms around each other and big smiles?"

You're thinking of the netball team, man. They're the huggers. The 'team' in 'athletics team' is silent. We just wear the same colour and share a minibus. Every one of us here is out for themselves. We run to win.

"High five!" she says. Like a cheerleader. But she's saying it to me. "High five!?" she says again, this time smiling and hand in the air. What sort of person would leave Minnie Michaels hanging?

. . . Me.

MINNIE

The photographer got some great shots of the netball team this morning so I'm pretty sure sports is covered, but the school is keen to showcase the range of sports teams in the new promo pictures, so I've changed kits and swapped my ponytail for a scruffy bun; maybe in a group shot it won't be as obvious it's the same face on both teams. None of the runners are interested in the photographer. I throw the poor guy a bone. "High five?" I offer to some of the girls. Lena Singleton doesn't hear me, she's focused on the track. She always is. I force a smile on an unsuspecting Year 7 – "High five!" she smiles, and as we clap hands, I hear the camera click.

"That's great, girls." He sounds relieved.

ALICE

When I say I run, I mean I walk quickly through the school gates, pulling my skirt down and tugging my blazer on and as far across my chest as it will go. I go straight to the bathroom and stare hard at my face. I back up and try and fit as much of my body as I can into the mirror. My boobs look big in this shirt. I can't see my bum or my legs but I know what they look like in this uniform. They look like they want attention, but that's hardly my fault. Where else can I put them? I zoom back into my face. My face is good. My skin is clear and my hair is cute. I just needed to be sure that I didn't accidentally turn into a pantomime dame on the way to school. That it wasn't my fault that some creep in a car mistook me for a lost member of a schoolgirl hen party. OK, I'm tall. OK, I'm . . . developed. Whatever. That guy was awful and ridiculous and he had no right to say those things to me. I straighten up and smile. I look nice. Smart and studious.

The top academic achievers/Nerds United photograph takes place in a cosy science classroom. The idea is, we're all sitting around a table, thrilled beyond belief that we've discovered fire and/or can work a Bunsen burner. I'm fully prepared to commit to the scene until I realise who the other members of this awkward family photo are.

There's me, my petite son, Jacob Porter, my petite daughter, Lucia Tan, my other petite daughter, Head Girl Tilda Jeffrey and a few of my other children who are so tiny I haven't bothered to remember their names. That smiley Australian guy isn't even *that* small, but it'd take a basketball team to make me look short.

I *was* sitting at the front of the shot, until the photographer realised I was blocking our beloved baby Bunsen flame (and all the other students) and should be moved to the back of the table so we could see everyone. And maybe I could sit down? And some of the others, yeah, actually, maybe *all* the others could stand, so no one thinks I'm the teacher, ha ha, why would a teacher be wearing a uniform though, ha ha ha, yeah, no problem, perfect . . .

By lunchtime I've decided that after today I might

never have my photograph taken ever again. Which is a shame because I do love a good selfie. On my way to the canteen, where I fully intend to tell Jodie and Caro about the horrendous guy in the car – the guy with The Face, the Head stops me in the corridor.

"Alice, I wonder if we could borrow you for just one more photo." Noooooo. ". . . Can you just run over to the new common room right now-ish."

I don't run. Also, nooooo.

". . . We just want to get a few lovely natural shots that show that friendships forged here are the real deal. Genuine. Built to last. That sort of thing. For the brochure. Do you mind?"

That is ridiculous. Of course I mind. "No problem, sir."

I haul myself into the common room, where I'm immediately stationed by a chair and told to start fake chatting to my new fake friends: two tiny, sporty girls. Presumably this is juxtaposition. One of them is the Australian's girlfriend, who introduces herself as Minnie. This is easy to remember because she is of mouse-like proportions. I have only ever known her as one of The Ponies (my nickname for her clan of relentlessly sporty girls with ponytails – she's the smallest one. I guess that makes her My Little Pony).

She also introduces her friend Lena, who gives us both a bit of a death stare. She's sporty too, but she's in a different gang – she sits with The Girls. You know, the ones officially designated as pretty enough for The Boys. The ones everyone thinks they want to be/be with. I almost introduce myself as Big Alice because I know that's what they think my name is, but I'm trying to move on from those bad vibes. I decide there's no point looking miserable in these photos so I try and get to know my new faux pals.

"What's your favourite cheese?"

They look confused. "Cheddar?" Minnie Mouse says.

"Why?" demands Lena.

"Oh, I just thought we could say the type of cheese, instead of the word 'cheese', when they take the photograph." I try and explain but the photographer shushes us. Weird, because he literally just said he wanted us to be chatting in the photograph.

"3-2-1, people!" he shouts.

"Camembert!" I say, as the flash goes.

"Cheese!" squeaks Minnie. The other one doesn't bother.

"Once more," the photographer calls out and instead of screaming, I throw back my head in raucous laughter. I like photographs of myself when I'm laughing – actually,

I probably like photographs of anyone when they're laughing. Almost anyone, not Hitler. Or The Face.

My hair rustles against Lena's face.

"Sorry," I say, wondering how many times today I've apologised for taking up space.

"No, it's fine." She allows me.

It's not though, is it? For me. None of this is fine.

When I finally catch up with my actual-by-choice-friends, I don't tell them about The Face at all. They're giggling about something that happened that time I wasn't there, but just like in the common room I find myself throwing back my head and laughing, because otherwise I. Might. Just. Scream?

LENA

The photos never end. There are the running shots. The mixing in the common room shots. Laughing with teachers. Leaning over shared homework with girls I don't have any classes with. Big Alice and Minnie Michaels. And because we look so convincing, we're called out for some more shots together. Three girls chatting on a damp bench. Three girls smiling next to the field. Three girls hilariously exiting the library. He wants us to chat in the dining room with no food on our plates. Ridiculous. At some point the bell goes and classrooms empty out. People linger on their way between lessons. A skinny guy with dark hair stops and openly gawps for a while. I assume he is staring at Minnie, but when the photographer's back is turned, I watch him sneak up on the tripod and check out the camera's credentials. Minnie is trying hard to make polite conversation with Alice, of course. Alice is loud, when she does speak, and I'm wondering if I've said anything at all, when I catch a glimpse of Aimee through a window. She's staring right at me and, just like I knew she would be, she's furious.

MINNIE

We get to skip the whole fourth period doing extra photographs. It's quite fun really, and definitely preferable to chemistry now that Daniel is in a different class. Netball events mean I'm quite used to the whole being-photographed-thing, but normally we actually look at the camera. Big team smiles! I have to physically stop myself standing up super straight and holding my hands crossed behind my back like we do in team photos. The photographer wants us to be in 'casual conversation with friends'. Except the friends I'm talking to aren't really my friends at all. Lena from athletics clearly just wants this to be over as soon as possible and I'm struggling a bit with the spontaneous fake chatting, but the tall girl, Alice, is really good at pretending to be laughing or whatever. She talks big and waves her hands around a lot, so I just smile back and hope that it makes a nice picture.

"That's great, thanks, girls. We've got some lovely photos today. You'll be able to buy extra prints if you want them. A nice keepsake of you and your friends, eh?"

And for some reason I say, "Oh yeah, thanks, that'd be lovely." Alice barely registers what he has said but I catch something flash across Lena Singleton's face. Something like pure disgust.

WE ARE RUNNING!
ARE YOU?

DISCOVER THE LIGHT WITHIN!

Local running club meets
6 p.m. at Ashton Park —
new members welcome.

Call Leo and get
FIT4LIFE: 07700 900 000

FIT4LIFE PT and Running Coach

PART ONE: WARM UP

ALICE

I feel a bit sick. Like something bad got into my system today and it's setting up camp in my tummy. The man in the car. I don't think I can ever listen to Britney Spears again! And then that humiliating photo shoot – it's really given me the ick. I want to run away from this day. Run away from the image of his horrid face. The Face – I keep picturing it but then I change the memory so he says different things to me. I imagine him calling me Big Alice. Ugh! Why is my brain being so cruel to me?! And then I think about how embarrassed I sounded when that photographer actually shamed me in front of my brainiac peers. Why did I say sorry to him!? Then I'm annoyed that I've been made to feel this way by people who don't even know me. I can't just sit with it. I can't sit still at all. My limbs are all twitchy and I just want to get away from this feeling . . .

So, I just decided about three minutes ago that I'm going to Do Somethin'! (Oops . . . I Did It Again! God, I loved Britney. I can't believe that FACE has ruined her for me.) I'm going to do something that I've never done before. And I'm going to do it right now.

I slip on my Vans and head for the front door. Philip is already waiting for me, beating his tail against the skirting board. He's a German Shepherd, by the way. The dog kind, not some enthusiastic European boyfriend.

"I'm taking Philip out!" I shout out to anyone who is listening. Mum and Dad shout out in unison from different floors.

"Thanks, pet."

Clara calls out from her bedroom doorway. "Can I come?"

"You are meant to be asleep." Mum and I are in sync now.

"I am asleep!" she shouts as she slams her bedroom door and scampers across her room. I hear her dive into her bed with a big thump. For such a small person, she is one big noise.

"Anyway, are you ready?" I say aloud . Maybe to Philip, more likely to myself. Because tonight, for the first time ever . . .

I am going for A Run.

MINNIE

Coach took me aside after practice tonight and said it was time to start thinking about my options. (I wish someone would tell me what they actually are.) He said I should "really consider a future in netball". I suppose, in my own way and without thinking about it for very long, I have considered it, and yeah, it makes sense to me. I know the competition will be tough, but everyone says I'm good enough and no one is saying that about me in any other subjects. I'm not dumb or anything, but I guess I'm average at maths, science, history, etc. Being average isn't much fun. I excel at two things: sport and being Daniel Turner's girlfriend.

Daniel moved to our school from Australia a year ago. I know it sounds made-up but it was love at first sight. That really happens! He's got these big brown eyes and curly brown hair and the biggest, whitest teeth you've ever seen. His smiles aren't just big. They're Australia big. He sat down on the table next to me and I honestly could not stop looking at him. I should have been embarrassed but he just smiled that extraordinary smile and said, "Hey, girl!" like we'd been friends for ages. I said "Hey, boy!" and then we had a few classes together and for a few months we said "Hey, girl!" "Hey, boy!" every day and sent "Night, girl!" "Night, boy!" messages at bedtime. After the summer he said "Hey, Girlfriend!" and I said "Hey, Boyfriend!" and our goodnight messages changed to "I love you".

We walk home holding hands. Daniel carries my kit and I munch a KitKat. He is telling me about a new climbing place he has heard about and he thinks we should go there in the summer holidays. It sounds like fun, and I am listening and nodding as he describes the videos he has watched online – but I'm also thinking about what Coach said. The county scouts will be attending some of our upcoming games. It is my chance to get noticed. "Things could happen" for me. What things? County things? National things? I guess that is what he meant by a future in netball. Me – going all the way to the top. Minnie Michaels, playing for England?

ALICE

Right, so I'm not going to run directly out of the house down my path or even down my road. I can't risk anyone seeing me, so I'm going to walk Philip to that shady alleyway that runs behind the posh houses and when we get there I'll start running. It's a nice long straight so I guess I'll just have to run up and down it a few times to make it a decent length. Maybe ten times? I don't know how long that will be. I should get one of those fitness watches that records my runs. Not that I'll share my stats online or anything, but it would be good for me to know if I am accidentally running a marathon every night after school. This is what I'm quite excited about – I've never really tried running before and what if I am naturally gifted at it? I do *look* sporty, what with all these long limbs, I just happen to not do any actual sport. Yet. From what I've seen on the Olympics, plenty of the long-distance runners are rocking the lanky look. Maybe running will just make perfect sense and my legs will be like, "FINALLY – this is what we were made for!"

If I'm that good at it then maybe I'll share my stats…

I walk past the care home but the games room is empty. I guess they're all in bed now but usually when I walk past all the grandmas and grandpas wave at me out the window and for some reason I always say out loud, "Say hello Philip", as if he understands that a room full of OAPs are waving at us. Sometimes I get him to jump up on to the wall to peep over so they can see I have a dog and I'm not just talking to myself or doing something odd like walking a ferret on a lead.

I've absolutely seen someone walking a ferret on a lead and let me tell you, that was one post that got a lot of likes. Even from the not-actually-my-friends-friends.

I walk past the shop and I consider going in to get some Lucozade or one of those mushed up fruit nut bars that Juliet eats when she is pretending to be healthy. Juliet is my auntie. She's thirty and awesome. I wonder if she goes running. She does wear a lot of Lycra. Maybe I will ask her for some tips or suggest we go for a run together and then she can buy me a smoothie at the gym cafe. She definitely goes there a lot but she only ever posts photos of the super-food salad she ate and not the actual workout.

Anyway, I'm going past all the houses with the posh names now – they're called 'Dunthwaite Holme' and 'Tamarisk Lodge' and one is just called 'Scruples' which must belong to some of those insanely rich people who are genuinely insane because that sounds like a dog or a hairdo and not a place to live. Do you have to put that on the envelope if you write to the people there? Do you say it when you order a taxi?

The posh houses end and the next turn is into the alley that I am going to run down. And back up again approximately ten times. Watch me now!

I don't go fully down like I'm on a starting block or anything but I do that half lean-in that the Olympians do, and off I go.

This.
    Feels.
        Amazing!

I am flying down this alleyway. I am so light on my feet! Who knew?!

Philip is loving it. He's smiling at me with hearts in his eyes. Look at his legs almost criss-crossing in the middle.

We are running machines. This *is* what our bodies were made for!

Ten laps will be over in minutes. We might have to make it twent-ER-OWWWWWHAT-THE-WHAT-IS-HAPPENING-TO-MY-INSIDES-MY-LUNGS-ARE-ON-FIRE!!!

I CAN FEEL MY TRACHEA! IT'S ALIGHT! IT'S BURNING! MY ENTIRE RESPIRATORY SYSTEM IS COMBUSTING!!!

I imagine the diagram of the respiratory system in my biology text book. The nose and ears and mouth all linked by red and blue lines that snake down the throat and spread out across the lungs in little twiggy offshoots and this is why THE FIRE IS SPREADING THROUGH MY WHOLE BODY SO QUICKLY. Obviously, I stop running to concentrate on dying a bit more. I lean on a fence and heave big exaggerated breaths. Forcing air into my blue lines. Or is it the red lines? Why didn't I bring a drink? I'm SO thirsty. Breathe breathe pant pant breathe. Breathe. Breeaaathe.

After some long breathy breathing I feel myself calming down. I look at Philip who is genuinely looking a bit concerned. I glance around to check if anyone saw what just happened. How I nearly died via self-inflicted exercise!

The coast is clear. I turn around and start to trudge home. Hopefully my face won't feel quite so burnt by the time we get back to civilisation.

No such luck. I am back outside the posh houses in less than thirty seconds, and Mrs Thornwoodthwaitington Palace is outside watering her creepers. I glance back down the alley to see how far I've "run".

I haven't even made it to the second lamp post.

No one notices that I come home looking cerise and depressed. Philip bounds straight through to the back garden as if the walk was just a warm up to playtime. Forget it, Phil, I'm going straight to bed.

My beloved Vans have rubbed through the skin on my big toe. I'm pretty sure when I take them off my toe will just be a wet stump, sanded down by my Old Skools. Note to self – wear proper running trainers next time.

Wait.

There's going to be a next time?

LENA

The alarm says 'SPRINTS!' and Dad says that means I'm meant to "Bolt out of bed". It's 5.30 a.m.

It's actually only an hour earlier than I get up every other day of the week but it feels like a different time zone. I never snooze the alarm though. That just makes it worse.

Dad meets me in the kitchen with a song and a banana. "The sun has got his hat on. Hip-hip-hip-hooray." Dad has got his hat on.

I've got my "do we have to?" face on. Me and my dad; we are not cut from the same cloth. I think I said *once* I wanted to improve my sprint-starts and Dad came up with this ridiculous weekly ritual. Wednesdays were the mornings he did his own training and he said if I was serious about running, he would go earlier so I could come too. I guess *he* was serious about me running so I went along and now that's what we do. Every week. Come rain or shine or period pain.

We walk over to the track. Our house backs on to the park, so it's just a few minutes' fast walking to warm up. Once we get there, we do a slow jog around the track to find our feet. We chat sometimes about what else we have going on that day. Dad is a personal trainer and he has clients every other morning, but not Wednesdays. He's also the coach of the local running club.

When we loop back around to the start line, we assume the position. I can't help but laugh. I know Dad is grinning at me. Wagging his finger at the sky and giving me the "Shhh" signal like his hero Usain Bolt used to do on the start line.

Get set.
        GO!

We push off and run as fast as we can to the 100m line. Arms pumping. Legs powering.

"Extend and run through the finish." It's hard. It hurts. Dad beats me easily every time but that isn't the point. He's running against himself. I'm running against me, apparently. Once we slow down, we turn around and walk back to the start line.

Get set.
> GO!
> Torture.

We do this eight times in a row. Each time I'm meant to give "everything" I've got to the sprint because "that's the point of sprinting", apparently. "To leave nothing behind." Dad says I will surprise myself a minute later by doing it all over again. That's what he loves about running. He says it makes him feel so strong when he realises he can dig a little deeper. It makes him feel proud.

It makes me feel sick.

But after our eight awful sprints we get to lap the track once more and head for home. I'm relieved it's over, and then I'm glad we did it. "You're a good coach, Dad." He is so happy and relaxed after the session he talks and talks. He makes me toast and eggs or sometimes pancakes. He makes me laugh.

ALICE

I try not to think about last night's horrendous "running" experience but it's difficult because I am already sort of obsessed with the idea of trying again. I must be remembering it wrong; it can't have been that bad. I'm sure I could have gone for longer. I just needed to try a bit harder. And wear different shoes. It was probably that. The trainers. They spoilt everything with their chunky flat-sole coolness. I didn't have any springy cushions or air pockets and my socks weren't football kit dri-fit stuff, they were just cotton ones with llamas on. No wonder it didn't work!

Jodie and Caro are waiting for me at lunch. We take our packed lunches to the field and find a spot to spread out. Caro always has the best lunch and she's quite happy to share, so I volunteer my ham sandwich as tribute and she gives me some of her sun-dried tomato couscous and one of her herby feta parcel things. Yummers. They're talking about something that happened in a class I'm not in. Loud boys are doing some obnoxious wrestling in the middle of the field. I guess we're watching, but more like when the Romans watched sports and hoped that everyone involved got hurt. The Girls are laughing as if The Boys are charismatic, and they whisper as if we care what they are saying.

I decided when I started high school that I would just avoid all *that* and, somehow, I've just about managed to. OK, I know I'm famous for being tall, but I don't get picked on for being a geek because I have friends who aren't. I don't have to worry about my eyebrows being on fleek for The Girls, I don't spend every after-school doing netball with The Ponies. I just sort of float about and to be honest it's pretty stress-free. I don't really get why TV makes high school look so ruthless. I sort of like it?

After lunch I have double art which is joyous. I sit with my fellow braniac, Jacob Porter. He is hilarious. But there are two Jacobs. Other Jacob sits on the other side of the classroom facing out of the window. From what I can tell from the back of his head, he is less hilarious than Jacob Porter. He genuinely has ebony black hair. Like Snow White. I imagine him washing dishes with woodland animals and singing songs with a bunch of dwarves.

We're all working on our exam coursework so we're allowed to listen to headphones in this class. Amazing. I love this because I can properly listen to stuff like podcasts or audio books without my little sister pulling out my earbud every two minutes to ask what I'm listening to now.

I'm not especially good at art, my ideas are definitely better than my execution, but I love the peace and quiet of the lessons. I wonder if this is what being a grown-up is like. Working in an office; just getting on with your tasks and listening to your headphones. Doesn't sound so bad to me. There is a lot of audio content out there.

At the end of the lesson I take my palette and brushes to the sink to wash out. Other Jacob comes over and empties his pencil shavings into the bin. His hands and cuffs are covered in lead. I steal a peek at his work on my way back to my desk. It's smudgy and shady and to be honest I can't really work out what it is that he has drawn. I look harder. Maybe it's like one of those magic eye pictures that you need to stare at until your eyeballs feel a bit fizzy but then suddenly you see a train or a shark jumping out to bite your face off. I step backwards in case that helps and stand on someone's toes. The Other toes, of course. Other Jacob is unlikely to find this hilarious. I look up at him and my fizzy eyes feel a bit watery. He probably thinks his shady goings-on have moved me to tears. I take a moment to de-fizz my eyes and pull his face into focus. His skin is . . . as white as . . . snow. His lips, the shade of the red, red rose – OK so they're just normal lip pink colour but he is quite pale and overall, he's sort of quite lovely. I've been staring too long now and my eyes have gone fizzy again. I attempt some sudden nonchalance and hum a little tune as I wander back to my desk.

. . . I'm humming 'Some Day My Prince Will Come'. *headdesk!*

LENA

We're spending our lunchtime watching the boys. Aimee, Nikki and Tasha are already in position. Near enough that we're definitely with them. Far enough away that we can talk *about* them. Sigh. They are *all* we talk about. I say 'we'; I mean Aimee talks and we agree. Tasha nibbles some Skittles but I need real food. Especially on a Wednesday. I'm ravenous by lunchtime but only Nikki wants to come to the canteen. "I need a drink," she says. I know she'll get some chips and I know she doesn't want Aimee to know. I get chips too. And lasagne, a salad, an apple and a Twix. "But you can get away with it." Nikki says, but it's really Aimee talking.

"It isn't a heist." I tell her, "It's just lunch."

Aimee and I have been friends since infant school. We acquired Nikki and Tasha when we joined high school. I think Aimee felt like we needed a crew or something.

I don't mind. On warm evenings we hang out at the park or the beach. Wherever the boys are. Athletics gets me out of some meet-ups. We have fun but I don't want to be a spectator every night. I don't really get how it's been decided that watching is all we do. The really dumb part is that I sit next to Sebastian Edwards in history, right before lunchtime. We talk the whole lesson and then get outside and split off into our gangs and barely make eye contact. I think Aimee 'likes' Sebastian. Tasha 'likes' Max. Aimee has decided that I should like Lewis. I don't 'like' Lewis. I don't not like Lewis. Who even is Lewis?

I'm off the hook today because after school I head straight to athletics. That's different to the running club my dad coaches but he's always asking what we're doing. He expects me to be the best, because he always was, despite there being no genetic reason for this to be a factor. I'm adopted, but he's raised me as if I were exceptional at everything. I've inherited his determination, at least. I'm better than average because I train hard, but I'm no Minnie Michaels. She's the one with running in her DNA. She beats me easily every time. Any time. She makes it look effortless. She's like my dad. She flies.

And she's the reason I don't run my dad's beloved 100m event at the inter-school meets.

I get to do the 400m because our club coach is a client of my dad's, but I know Minnie could beat me in that event too. Dad says I just need to keep practising and I'll get there.

"Keep pushing," he says.

Stop pushing, I think.

Minnie isn't too focused on sprinting, thankfully. I think her focus this year is netball. I heard she's the best the school has ever seen. I heard she's going pro. I heard she's all anyone ever hears about.

Dad's coming to pick me up and I don't want to be seen on track at the same time as Minnie so I'm heading to the sand pit. Maybe I can be the best at triple jump or something.

MINNIE

I'm watching a film with Daniel and his parents. My phone is pinging with messages from the netball team. They're chatting about our big game next week. It's 'our' big game but Captain Bella says it's *my* BIG game. Capital letters B-I-G because the county scouts will be there. She's being sweet, I'm sure they will be checking her out as well, but I move the conversation on quickly and remind them about all the fun we'll have on the bus. That's everyone's favourite bit really. The McDonalds and the singing and the selfies. Bella always gets a Chicken McNuggets meal with a side of Chicken McNuggets. Goalkeeper Sophie sends the boomerang of Bella's McNugget dance and then the next six pings are emojis and LOLZ.

Bella and Sophie are the only girls in the club team who also go to my school. We all play for the school team too, for fun, but the club is serious stuff. There are some social hang-outs with the club, but I don't tend to go to many. They tease me about it, but it's only banter.

Dear everyone except Minnie who can't make it, let's go to the cinema/the shopping centre/the park after training this weekend.

I can't make it because I already have plans with Daniel. I know I should be all 'friends before boyfriends', but they're mostly just 'the team' to me. I guess I didn't really have a best friend before Daniel so no one was put out when he came in. The team understand, they just make jokes about it and then privately tell me they would love to have a relationship like mine. I always say 'well it could happen with [insert name of their crush]' but I'm not sure I believe it. Lots of people at school say they're going out with someone but as far as I can tell they never actually go out anywhere. I know it's special with Daniel.

The film ends with the boy and girl getting back

together after a series of dramas that probably would never have happened if they just talked to each other properly. There was some crying and walking in the rain in the middle and those montages of happy times and sad times to show weeks passing. I get a bit bored in these sorts of films. I know how it ends and honestly, I could do without the bit in the middle. I want to know the couple stay together but I don't want to go through the stressful bits where I'm meant to believe they won't. I suppose it wouldn't make much of a movie, but aren't there any times when it just works and no one misses their plane or picks up a letter meant for someone else or gets run over trying to cross the street. I'm not asking for a friend . . .

Daniel's parents busy themselves tidying away our cups and snacks so we can say goodbye privately. They don't leave us too long.

"Are you sure I can't walk you home?" Daniel's smile is whole-continent-wide.

"Go and do your homework!" I say. If he walks me home, we'll spend another half hour saying goodbye at my door too and I'm always keeping one eye on making sure I don't interfere with Daniel's schoolwork. He's going to get into a top university. He'll walk his exams, but he does need to get on with his coursework and he's easily distracted. Especially by me. I heard his mum say it once.

"Homework! Now!" I say again for his mum's benefit. She has wandered through from the kitchen to check we're still in PG territory.

"Night, girl," he says with a wink.

"Night, boy," I say over my shoulder as I start down the path. I hear the door close behind me and I fasten the gate. I get out my phone before it pings. I know it will.

Daniel: Love you, girl

I'm smiling at my phone as if it was his lovely face, and that's when I get run over trying to cross the street.

ALICE

I get up from the dining table and give Philip the nod. He has no idea what I mean so he sits up and does the wag-and-whine. Excited and confused and frustrated all at once. Same, boy.

"I'll take him out, shall I?" I say casually as I clear some plates away.

"Mmmhmm," Mum says as she retrieves the fish fingers, chips and peas that Clara has catapulted on to the carpet. Must remember to check my hair for ketchup.

"Go and wait by the door, Phil. I'll grab some shoes," I say in that way that totally guilty people talk when they are giving a false alibi. It's not even a lie. I do go and grab some shoes, they're just not mine. Mum's bouncy Zumba trainers are only half a size too big but I pad them out by wearing some of Dad's football socks. The heel might be half way up the back of my calf but I'm sure this high-tech fabric will make me run faster. I've got poo bags (for Philip!!) and my phone in one pocket, and a bottle of water in the other. Actually, it's one of Clara's little sippy cups with a pop-up straw, but a litre of Evian is hardly going to fit in my fleece.

We head for the same destination. Philip seems to know the plan. He's intuitive like that. When we pass 'Scruples' I start to get butterflies. I've definitely convinced myself that last time was just a bad dream and this time is going to be astronomically different, in that it won't be a catastrophe and no part of my body will catch fire.

I start slowly. Really slowly. I'm probably just walking but they have that on the Olympics now too; it's definitely a sport. I'm focusing on why I want to do this. How I'm going to reclaim my body and maybe the ability to enjoy the work of Britney Spears. I fast-walk the space between the first three lamp posts and then I run to the fourth. I *am* going to be 'Stronger than yesterday'. I keep going and run to the fifth post. I set off for the sixth and become a fire-breathing dragon again. I wonder if I have asthma. I definitely have water though, so I gulp it down and then I bravely go back to fast walking. I've got my first stitch. I always wondered why they were called that. It's because it feels like someone is stabbing you with a giant needle and sewing up your ribs so you can't breathe.

I solider on with my fast walking to lamp posts seven and eight and then I slow down to a hobble and then I just stop. Crikey it hurts. I glug more water and the bottle is empty already. I've seen other people do this. Why does that bloke in Lycra shorts who jogs past our house never look like he's dying from the inside out? How is running this hard and why do so many people do it when it feels this hideous? I feel a bit outraged. Like this is some sort of conspiracy. I can feel my face burning. I imagine sirens in the distance. My breathing is ridiculous. I'm in shock. The emergency services must be coming for me. Someone has witnessed me, crumpled up like junk mail, and they've called 999. It almost feels like a reasonable response until I shamble around the corner and see an actual emergency. The sight of a girl lying in the road jolts me back into the world that has other people in it. Someone is hurt and it isn't me.

I take in the scene as I find myself jogging(!) over to see if I can help (on what basis, I have no idea). For some reason, I can't bring myself to look at the girl on the floor, instead I search the faces of the people who love her and I'm surprised to see that I know one of them. My almost-regular-sized brainiac acquaintance, Australian Daniel. I guess, this is what he looks like when he isn't smiling from ear to ear. And I guess, that makes the girl on the floor my fake friend from the photographs, Minnie Mouse.

"I don't know what I can do, but can I help!?" I say as a way of distancing myself from a person who has just come to gawp, like the old dear next door craning over her garden wall. At least come out to the gate, Grandma.

Australian Daniel glances up to meet my eye but he doesn't recognise me or he doesn't care at this moment in time. Fair enough.

The people I assume to be his parents step forward and probably-Daniel's-mum says "Thanks love, the ambulance is already on its way," and then I am sure she is his mum because she sounds like Mummy Kangaroo from Peppa Pig (Clara watches it, OK?).

"I go to school with Daniel and Minnie," I add.

Just to stress the not-gawping vibe and then I guess because Daniel won't let her and she's upset too, Mrs Mummy Kangaroo sweeps me into a quick hug.

"Oh, love, come here, she'll be all right, I know she will," she says over my head.

She releases me and I step away and hope that Daniel doesn't choose this moment to say 'actually, Mum, I barely know this person' and I make myself look at her.

Minnie, on the road. Someone has put her in the recovery position and I feel a flash of relief that I wasn't first on the scene. I make a mental note to learn how to do that later. She looks like she's asleep and I stare at her until I'm sure I've seen it with my own eyes; she's definitely breathing. Daniel is crouched over her and his dad is crouched over him. It's a chain of reassuring arm rubs and I think about rubbing Mummy Kangaroo's arm when the ambulance swoops around the corner.

The moment erupts into a clatter of doors and voices, paramedics in green and fluoro-yellow with questions and poor Daniel trying to answer them and ask his own and get in the van and wipe those tears from his eyes. Daddy Kangaroo remembers I'm there and turns around.

"Thanks, love," he says, instead of goodbye.

As I trudge home, I can't stop thinking about Minnie

lying in the road. Little Minnie Mouse lying in that ambulance. She's some sort of sports star. I bet she goes running all the time. Maybe she was going out for a run right then and now she can't. What's my excuse? It's my duty to myself, and now to Minnie, to make this work. If there is a secret to running, I just need to find out what it is . . .

Ok, Google How do I learn to run?

GREGAN VALE
NETBALL CLUB

VS

BARTON BELLES
NETBALL CLUB

Regional Semi-Final

Saturday, 1 p.m.
Stanley Park,
Court Two

COME ON, GIRLS, YOU CAN DO IT!

PART TWO: THE CHASE

LENA

The main headline is that Minnie Michaels has been hit by a car. That's all we know so far. I'm hearing different takes in every corridor. She's broken her neck. She's brain-dead. She's limping. She's fine. I wouldn't wish a serious injury on anyone, but the limping story wouldn't be SO bad . . .

Aimee doesn't care about Minnie Michaels' accident. "Skinny Minnie – boo hoo!" We're just standing in the playground people-watching when my other fake friend from the photos walks past us and Aimee spies a change of topic.

"Nikki . . . what do you think of Big Alice's figure?"

Aimee drops this question casually, but it's like dropping the pin from a grenade. The silence is loaded. I'm curling my toes already because this can only go one way for Nikki. Aimee has already decided what she thinks about Alice's figure and now Nikki has to work out what the correct answer is. If she says it's good, she might be called a lesbian (which in Aimee's silly world is a burn). If she says it's bad, Aimee will claim Alice has the best figure in school. And then probably find a way to tell Alice that Nikki thinks she's fat.

The other thing is, Nikki *is* a little bit fat. So there's a 'well, you can talk' comment hanging in the air as well.

Nikki is looking at us for help.

"I wish I had legs as long as hers," I hear myself say. Nikki visibly relaxes and Aimee shoots lasers with her eyes. "I'd finally beat Minnie Michaels!"

Nikki laughs, probably more out of maniacal relief than humour.

Aimee hooks her arms through Tasha's in a huff. As she steers her away, I hear her saying, "Big Alice is a total freak. Imagine wanting to look like that!?"

Tasha laughs. Nikki looks close to tears and I don't feel far off myself. Longer legs wouldn't even help me beat Minnie.

MINNIE

So, I've broken my shoulder. A silent cyclist came whizzing down Daniel's road just as I stepped out between two parked cars. He crashed into me and I fell and now I'm in a sling for anything from two to eight weeks, pain dependent.

On the bright side; no surgery, no pins. Not even a long stay in hospital. I should be home tomorrow. I had a bit of concussion and a headache that lingered but I feel mostly fine today so, fingers crossed, this is my last hospital 'pasta bake'. I do like this hospital ice cream though. It's nowhere near frozen so it's just like eating a tiny foamy vanilla milkshake with a Sylvanian Families spoon. Daniel brought me some grapes in a brown paper bag (he saw on a cartoon that that's what you take when you visit people in hospital), but they're just going soft on my nightstand.

The team have been messaging me sad faces. No one has mentioned the fact that I'm obviously not going to be able to play the regional semi-finals. That I'll miss the scouts. That this stupid fracture might have cost me my whole netball career, before it even started. Everyone is working really hard to not mention that.

Except the doctor. Who told me that my shoulder *should* heal beautifully. I'm young and it's a clean fracture and the lasting damage *should* be minimal. I shouldn't worry about having a stiff shoulder *for the rest of my life.* And I hadn't been, until he said that. Physical therapy can help me with "anything like that" he says. *Anything like that.* Anything like being uncomfortable for the rest of my life. Anything like losing out on all the plans I've made that revolve around me having a strong shoulder? He doesn't know about netball and athletics and the climbing wall with Daniel, so he doesn't mention returning to sports or how my performance might have been affected. I can't bring myself to ask.

He says, "when it stops hurting, you'll be able to move it as normal."

What do normal people do with their shoulders?

"Hey, girl."

Daniel walks in and I burst into tears.

"Babe, no! What's wrong?" I wonder if this is the first time he's ever seen me cry.

Between gulps I manage to say, "It's ... just ... netball!" and then I wail. Like a toddler. *Waah.* I want to play netball and I can't.

"It's ... not ... fair!"

I can't believe I said that out loud but that's what it is. Not fair. No one's fault. No one else's problem. Nothing I can do or say to change it. I didn't do anything wrong or bad to deserve it (if you'll forgive me the whole

Stop! Look! And Listen! thing). It's just not fair. And I've got to live with it for the next two to eight weeks.

Pain dependent.

ALICE

Sarah, on the RunTime app, is going to be my coach. She says if I follow her plan, I'll be able to run for around thirty minutes non-stop in nine weeks' time. Sarah is really optimistic about this. She's already proud of me for making the decision that I want to run. Thanks, Sarah.

We're going to run three times a week! And she says I should try and take 'rest days' between my 'sessions'. Like a proper runner. She also said that I don't need to invest in any flashy trainers or sports clothes but I have seen some sporty leggings in big Tesco that weren't too expensive. Maybe I can sneak them into the trolley next week. If I'm going to be running three times a week for nine weeks, I should look the part. I'm pretty excited. Sarah really thinks I can do this!

Philip and I are en route to the alley. Let's hope there are no ambulances this time, for me or anyone else. I send quick good thoughts to Minnie Michaels. I'll switch Sarah on when we get there. It's like we're friends meeting up for a run. Oh yeah, me and my

BFF Sarah, we run together three times a week. Right, Hello, 'Scruples'. Hello, Nemesis Alley and tricksy lamp posts that get further away as you run towards them. I'm not counting you anyway. My running buddy Sarah is going to get me through it. Let's do this!

Oh, so the first thing we're going to do is walk for ten minutes to warm up. I sort of did that already walking here. Come on, Sarah, catch up.

I whizz forward for ten minutes. Right. Running bits. We're going to run for twenty seconds and then I get to walk again for two whole minutes. Sounds all right. Is Sarah going a bit tame on me? I mean, I have been on two runs before . . . On my marks. Get myself set. Go!

Geeez-Louisiana, one of my lungs has already collapsed and Sarah just had the nerve to say we were "halfway there".

Sarah is a cow. Twenty seconds is an age.

But it's done and now we get to walk and chat for two minutes. She says I did really well. I guess I did. I didn't stop. Even when I really wanted to; she said we only had four seconds left and then it was three, two, one and I had done it. At the end of this two minutes we're going to do it again and she says it will feel easier every time. If that's true then my worst run will always be behind me!

On the other hand (foot), when I do my next run, that one will be my new worst run.

But also, my best!

Good grief, Sarah, you're giving me a headache and now we have to run again so I'd better say goodbye to my other functioning lung . . .

Philip bounds through the door as happy as an elf on Christmas morning and I stagger behind him like a reindeer who has pulled an all-nighter. Sarah said I should have a proper dinner with lots of vegetables to refuel my body after a run. She might be talking more about the weeks at the end of the programme where we're running for more than a total of 100 seconds but no one said anything about earning more food the longer you run so it's pie and mash with loads of veg and a side of HELL YEAH!

That night, I collapse into my bed and wonder if my limbs will hurt tomorrow. That's called DOMS (Delayed Onset Muscle Soreness) and it's why I need a rest day. I've earned it. I completed my first session. I really am going to learn how to run.

LENA

I won! I smashed it. OK, so Minnie Michaels wasn't there. But, the thing is, she won't be back any time soon. She's broken her elbow or her arm or her shoulder – we're still not quite sure – but she's broken. She won't be running for the rest of this term. Apparently, it's a major blow for her netball club and our school team. She can't run. And I can. And I'm feeling fast.

I wish Dad could see me. The other girls look sluggish in my dust. We run 800m, 400m and even some of the dreaded 100m races. I win everything. Sprinting is still hard but it feels so much better when you win. It won't make Wednesday mornings any easier, but if I knew I was training with a chance of winning maybe I'd get more into it. Dad would be so happy if I was a winner.

Mr Day, the PE teacher who co-ordinates the after-school clubs, congratulates me on a great session. I look around for someone to high five but the other runners aren't that interested in my wins. I realise I don't even know their names. I guess I don't really interact much with the others.

Minnie Michaels wasn't just faster than me . . . she was crushing my spirit.

MINNIE

Sitting still is driving me nuts.

I'm taking a few weeks off school because I'm still really sore and I'm having trouble sleeping which makes me a zombie in the daytime. Captain Bella drops some homework off for me to do but I don't really look at any of it. I'm bored and tired and grumpy. I can't go to the gym. I can't even start physio until I finish my pain medication and I'm out of the sling. I just stare at my phone, hoping it will ring but with no idea of who I'd like it to be.

I honestly don't know what to do with myself.

Mum doesn't know what to do with me either. She tries to talk to me but I'm not really in the mood for heart-to-hearts, and when I do let her sit down she quickly gets annoyed that two minutes of her sympathy hasn't solved everything and I'm still upset. She offers me a lot of toast and I keep accepting it because at least I can do that. She's offered to take me to the nail salon for a pick-me-up-pedicure, but no one ever sees your toes when you live in trainers . . . lived in trainers.

I know, I'm really dramatic. Daniel's being low-key about it. He just says it'll be fine. I'll still be the best player by a mile next season and I'm not going to miss anything.

I think he's probably right but I also can't shake the feeling that I'm missing something huge. Like this was my time to shine. It's just netball, I know, but I think there's only a small window to be great at something. And you have to squeeze through that window at the moment when everything fits just right, and then it lets you into another world where that's the norm. Does that make sense? Maybe this was going to be *my* moment, and I'm missing it.

ALICE

OK, I am cheating, but not in the way you think, oh ye German Shepherd of little faith. No, no, Philip. We're going to go out again . . . tonight! I don't need the rest day. I want to run with Sarah again tonight. I've looked up the podcast online to see how the programme progresses and it's a whole week of doing these really short bursts of running with a lot of walking, and I feel fairly confident I can do that without needing a day off in between. I owe it to Minnie Michaels to crack on with this. Let's just smash these beginner bits and get on with the actual running, already!

Back from my run. It started raining and that awful cow Sarah increased the run to twenty-five seconds so I've fallen out with her. I'm going to take that rest day tomorrow so I can blank her.

At school the next day, Caro and Jodie are talking about something hilarious that happened in class before lunch. Their classes are always hilarious it would seem. You wouldn't think there would be that many opportunities for giggles in Social Studies, but whatevs. I guess you have to be there. I had English, and there were actually some good jokes in *The Taming of the Shrew* but I'm not sure they'll work as well over a Coke and a Twix.

"What were you up to last night?" Caro is looking at me now. "You didn't read our messages for ages!"

"Oh, sorry, I was just out walking Philip." Not a lie.

"Ah, yeah."

Our chat group always has loads of messages, but quite often it's the two of them talking about things I've missed. Or filling me in on plans they've already made for the three of us. It's not a big deal, they don't do it intentionally, it's just annoying that they always make their plans during lessons I'm not in. And then it's already in motion and I'm left out before it even starts because I'm busy being a swot in Swotsville class with all the nerds.

To be honest, hardly anyone in my classes is even remotely nerdy. They're just normal and decent at exams, I reckon. That's all anything is based on at school. How well you cope in an exam situation. It's not like the lessons are particularly different, or the subjects are suddenly harder because you're in set one instead of set two. They can't make learning about factory life in Victorian England more or less difficult, can they? They can probably make it more or less boring. And apparently, they can make it more or less amusing. Anyway, I've just had the opportunity to tell my BFFs about my secret running habit and instead I sort of lied to them because I'm not even sure I am their BFF any more. They are each other's BFF and my BFF is Philip, and possibly podcast Sarah.

Screw rest day. Come back, Sarah, all is forgiven . . .

MINNIE

This week has been difficult. Or rather, this week *I've* been difficult. My shoulder doesn't even hurt that much any more but I feel stressed the whole time. I am constantly googling how long it should take to heal and how soon I can get back to netball. I keep trying to rephrase the question so I get the answer I want, which is just go back now and it will be OK. I hear myself snapping at Mum. I give the bare minimum in the team's chat group. It's not that I think they'll be mean or anything, the opposite in fact. They will be super encouraging and it will be super annoying because for some reason I can't shake this super bad mood I'm in. My phone pings again and I genuinely roll my eyes. I have no energy to respond. It's just chat. They aren't really *saying* anything.

I give Daniel the night off from yet another movie and popcorn with my parents. I know he's got coursework to do. I let Mum pick the film. I don't even care what it is. They're all rolling into one. Sometimes I nod off a little but only for long enough to miss some vital part of the story and render the rest of the film totally incomprehensible. Then I go to bed and don't sleep.

Mum has picked a French film starring one of her favourite actresses. She says it can count as doing some French homework and laughs, but to be honest it is genuinely the closest I'll have come to doing any school work. From what I can gather, it's just a sort of sad story about a woman who is unhappy with her life.

I think she lost her job or something, but I'm messaging Daniel at the same time and I keep missing parts of the conversation. France looks nice. Paris is so pretty. I bet you feel like you're in a film just walking down the banks of the river. The French actress looks incredibly chic just in jeans and a plain shirt, in the way that only really very tall, slim, rich people can. I look down at my trackie bottoms and wonder what I'll wear when I'm a grown-up.

I can't imagine any part of me as a grown-up. It's just occurred to me that when I imagined my life as a netball player, I was only ever the age I am now – living at home with my mum and dad and wearing my hair in a ponytail.

The French lady is sitting in a Parisian cafe, alone, with a book. The rain is pouring down outside and she stops the waiter to order an espresso and, weirdly, some vanilla ice cream. It's hard to imagine this lady doing anything that wasn't painfully stylish but this addition of ice cream seems a little bit quirky. Is she having a breakdown in the film and I've missed it?

The coffee and the ice cream arrive and the lady, in her silk shirt and tailored blazer, tips the little cup of coffee all over her scoop of vanilla ice cream. She eats the whole thing with a teaspoon and she looks like she really, really enjoys it.

I put down my phone and watch the rest of the film and honestly, not much happens in it at all. I can see why Mum likes the actress so much though. She is cool, in the true sense of the word. Suddenly, being French seems like the coolest thing in the world. It also feels like worlds away from whatever I am. The vanilla ice cream feeling sours in me and I feel angry again. Angry that I've never watched this French film before. Angry that it didn't occur to me to apply for the French exchange. Angry that I've never owned a pair of skinny jeans.

"Do you want some toast, darling?" Mum says, and I almost shriek back at her, "No!"

I call Daniel. "I need to get out."

LENA

I get home to an empty house. Dad is out with a client. Usually I'd use this an excuse to hog the bathroom for hours. Soak in the tub. Play some music. Eat Maltesers. But tonight, I feel pumped. I can't sit still. I want to race again. I want to win again. I need to make sure it really happened. That I am fast.

I chomp on some cashew nuts and change into some fresh gear. Clean socks always make me feel refreshed.

I grab my headphones and head out the door. I'm not sure where I'm going or how long I'll be. I've just got to move. Half of me hopes Dad will come back while I'm out and I can tell him I've been for a run. He'd love that.

I head out the door and I'm about to start a light jog when Sebastian and Max turn the corner.

"Hey," Sebastian calls out.

"Hi, Seb. Hi Max."

Aimee would love this. It's her dream to casually bump into Seb outside of school. If she looked perfect, of course. I don't think she'd count my leggings and vest as being meet-cute ready. I couldn't care less what he thinks of my outfit. I'm not out to impress Sebastian or Max, and if Lewis was here, I wouldn't be trying to impress him either.

"Where are you off to?" Sebastian always has a cheeky glint in his eye.

"I was going out for a run," I say, feeling proud, even though I hadn't actually run yet.

"Don't do that. Come for a burger with us instead!"

"What?!" I say. I don't need this repeating, it's just not what I expected him to say.

"Yeah, come on. Didn't you already have athletics

tonight? That's enough running. Come to BurgerShack. Your friends are going to be there anyway."

I am hungry . . .

Sebastian laughs as he steers me in the opposite direction from wherever I was going to run. Max doesn't say anything and as I let myself be dragged towards BurgerShack I realise I'm not just hungry, I'm ravenous. I start mentally preparing my order as we're walking through the door.

Aimee and Tasha are there, and Nikki is not. Considering I wasn't even aware of this plan, I think the idea was that this would fall into double-date territory. They wanted to increase their chances of getting the boys' attention, and now I'm here and I've ruined everything. I get dagger eyes from Aimee before I get my hug. Nice way to greet your friends.

"Look who I found!" Seb says proudly. "She's done some mad running and now she needs loads of fries."

"That's actually true," I say. Wondering how I'm going to apologise later. A bit annoyed because I shouldn't have to. Resigned to the fact I will.

"Cool, let's order!" Max says.

"I'm so hungry," Tasha says. She orders a Diet Coke and a small fries and brings another Diet Coke for Aimee.

They share the fries.

"I'm going to order," I say when they get back, hoping I can show Aimee and Tasha that I'm not trying to get any alone time with either of the boys.

"Me too!" says Seb, jumping up. Annoying timing, doofus.

I order everything. Well, a burger, fries, a side of chicken, a milkshake.

"That sounds good, same for me," Sebastian is really trying to drop me in it.

We take our matching orders back to the table and I make him slide into the booth next to Aimee. I perch at the head of the table, crashing the double date and eating my mega meal as quickly as possible. My plan is to make my excuses and grab an ice cream to go.

Sebastian won't stop talking to me. He keeps laughing about stuff we talk about in class and I wish he wouldn't do that. Aimee doesn't need to know that we sit together. She definitely doesn't need to know we have things we laugh about. She's angry, I can tell, and my heart sinks when Lewis walks in. She's going to say something embarrassing; I can feel it before it even happens.

But it doesn't happen. Sebastian jumps up to see Lewis, bouncing off like a happy puppy. Max mutters something under his breath and goes off to join them too, and suddenly we're just the girls again.

"I didn't know you were such good pals with Seb," Aimee says. Here we go.

"I'm really not," I begin, the milkshake curdling in my stomach. But then, amazingly, something else gets her attention.

"Oh my god, look who it is . . ."

ALICE

I'm being stalked. By the paparazzi. But singular. A paparazzo.

I was out with Sarah. On my own this time. I told Mum I was just going to the shop for some emergency CDM (Cadbury's Dairy Milk) and she was so delighted by this idea that she didn't say anything along the lines of 'but Tesco is at least twenty-five minutes' walk away and it's nearly dark and you are my first born, light of my life, apple of my eye and I must protect you at all costs so I will drive you because we also need milk.'

She did say the thing about needing milk though, so I did actually have to go to the shop. But I was going running so it didn't matter that it was a twenty-five minute walk because I was going for my thirty minute run-walk and I'd be there and back in no time.

I dismissed a "Whatsssuuuppppp" from Jodie and Caro on my phone. I knew I had to fit in all the running part before I got to the shop (can't run with hands full of milk and CDM) so I fast-forwarded the warm-up walk and went straight in for the first run. It was thirty seconds and to be honest, it wasn't complete torture.

The second and third and fourth runs were, of course, but I did them and I think I got my breath back a little quicker in between. I spent less time thinking I was drowning in fresh air and thought a little bit more about my feet striking the ground. How they were moving me forward and there was even a tiny glimpse of me imagining going a little bit quicker. I thought about Minnie Michaels and how she was in bandages and I was not, because a few Peppa Pig plasters on your toes do not count. I could see the shop in the distance and I knew there were two more runs before the cool down walk. I decided to give it everything I had in the penultimate run to see if I could get to the shop on my final burst, but actually the shop came towards me a lot quicker than I expected once I started running at it and then, out of nowhere, a photographer popped out of the darkness and took my photo.

Sarah says I can have one minute of walking before my final run and I am so shocked by what has just happened that I stop altogether and say 'WHAT?' aloud, to myself, but I know I shout it because I always do when I'm wearing headphones. I have a quick flashback of The Face and I shudder. I start to feel scared and then I remember that I'm angry. I'm angry at The Face and the school photographer and now I'm angry at whoever thinks they have the right to take photographs of me when I'm doing my private running that no one knows about. This is *my* secret running club and it is no place for anyone who wants to make me feel bad about myself. I look around to see if I can spot the slimy paparazzo, because I'm ready to give him a piece of my mind, but I have run for another ten seconds since then and the cameraman is probably choking on my dust. Serves him right.

My phone pings with more chat from my friends, but telling them about the photographer means telling them about running, and telling them about running, means telling them about The Face, and this whole drama is just too long to type out right now . . . or something.

I listen to Sarah talk me through the final run as I walk around Tesco Express. She is so encouraging. "Come on, this is your last twenty-five seconds of effort." I open the fridges. "You can do it!" Pick up some milk. "You're doing brilliantly." Locate the CDM. "One last push!" Select the family-size bar. "Smashed it!"

I use the self-service till so I can keep Sarah talking. It is so nice to have someone congratulate me while I complete my transaction, which, to be fair, does deserve a congratulation because you usually need assistance approximately fourteen times more than you would have if you'd just gone to the cashier – but only people who want to buy booze or fags go to the cashier.

Sarah starts the cool-down walk as I am paying up and we set off home together with my new calcium-heavy weights, for an extra arm workout.

I look out for the mystery photographer on my way back but, of course, there's no one to be seen. Sarah's voice is very relaxing now and rethinking it, I bet it was someone taking a lovely scenic photograph that I just happened to run into. That is a totally plausible explanation. The sunset is a little bit #beautiful.

Mystery solved. I crack open the CDM to congratulate myself but as I'm holding the milk in my other hand, I have to just bite off chunks as I walk. God, I hope there isn't a paparazzo lurking in the bushes now because being snapped walking home munching on a family-size bar of chocolate in my mum's trainers with a beetroot face and sweaty hair is definitely not #beautiful.

I get home and Mum takes the milk and the chocolate off my hands at the door. She doesn't notice the sweat or the trainers but she does notice that I didn't take Philip and he could probably do with a little trot round the block before bed . . .

MINNIE

We're in BurgerShack. I'm hiding my strapped-up shoulder under a giant hoody and I'm hiding my face under some unwashed hair and Daniel's baseball cap. He says I look beautiful. He's full of it. He claims he hasn't washed his hair either, but of course his curly mop looks 100% adorable. A fast-food place isn't exactly a Parisian cafe but I guess there is vanilla ice cream and probably some sort of coffee here if I wanted to order it. I'm trying to put that out of my mind. It's a really dumb thing to be annoyed about – not being middle-aged and French. I'm here to be with Daniel. Whatever I'm getting wrong, it isn't him. His phone has just buzzed and he is laughing with whoever is on the line. Something cruel reminds me that the only person I laugh with on the phone is him. I tune out of that thought because my ears have picked up on something else . . .

"Is that really her?"

"It can't be, she looks awful!"

"Well, I heard she had concussion. Clearly she's forgotten how to use mascara."

". . . or a hairbrush!"

Someone is whispering about me and not very quietly. Daniel has finished his call but remains completely oblivious to this conversation behind me. Now that I've tuned into it, I can't turn their volume down. Whatever Daniel is saying to me is drowned out by this catty gossip that I should not pay attention to.

"Who is it behind me?" I ask Daniel to peek over. I have to know.

"Some girls." He is hopeless.

"Come on, Daniel. They're from our school. You probably have classes with them."

"I don't think I do."

Fair enough. I'll have to steal a glance myself.

It's Lena from the athletics team! I can't believe it. What has she got against me? Although I would have recognised her voice, I think. Maybe I wouldn't. She never really says much. She's with two other girls. One of them I know is Tasha, who is in one of my classes, and the other one is Aimee something. I think she said the thing about me looking awful. She has that cruel look about her. She's pretty but she's angry, and somehow it's visible even when she's smiling. I don't know why it would be directed at me like that though. She doesn't even know me. I can't believe this group of girls are meeting up over milkshakes to say mean things about me.

I need to get out of here before I cry. How am I this bothered? I agree, my hair does need a brush but why have they even noticed?

Does it sound naïve to say it has never occurred to me before that anyone would ever say mean things about me? Not because I think everyone loves me, but because I didn't know I would register as a point of interest. Not only am I on their radar, I'm offending them! I need to get out of here now, but I don't want Daniel to notice that they've upset me. He might say something.

"Shall we go?" I say.

"Sure," he says. He holds the door open for me and then laces his fingers through mine. I am trying to work out if I'm more upset that Lena and her friends made fun of my hair, or that they have never invited me out for a burger.

LENA

My mega meal tastes pretty epic but I do feel a little queasy afterwards. I can't tell if that was the side of spicy chicken wings or the other thing that happened.

So, we spot Minnie and her goofy boyfriend at the burger place. They are always together when she's not on the track or on the court or in the pool or any of the other places she wins everything. I think they have one of those genuine grown-up relationships. It's not like they hold hands in the playground while talking to their friends but never actually speak to each other. They're a real couple. They are there and I think Minnie has some sort of sling on but her arm is hidden under a jumper. It is a really big jumper and she wears a baseball cap. I wear baseball caps sometimes too, but I don't think Minnie usually does. Anyway, Aimee decides that Minnie looks bad.

She doesn't. She just doesn't look her usual picture-perfect self. Which is probably still better than most but Aimee sees the window of opportunity and jumps straight through it.

"Oh my god, look who it is!"

Tasha isn't even sure it is Minnie at first. "Is that really her? . . . It can't be, she looks awful."

Aimee is loving it. "Well, I heard she had concussion. Clearly she's forgotten how to use mascara."

I guess I am still buzzing about my good practice because I hear my own voice say ". . . or a hairbrush!"

Aimee gives me this look. Eyes ablaze with something like joy or evil. She high fives me and for some reason we laugh and laugh and laugh.

THE SUMMER BALL IS JUST AROUND THE CORNER

Tickets must be paid
for in full by this Friday.

NB: The school art exhibition will be on display for the Summer Ball
— please see Miss Hallam for details on how to submit a piece.

PART THREE: THE OVERTAKE

LENA

I know what I'm doing. I see myself. And yet, I'm not stopping it.

I said that thing about Minnie Michaels' hair and suddenly I am Aimee's favourite again. It's like a switch has been flipped and we are nine years old again.

That night, after BurgerShack, she suggested we go and get doughnuts at what she knows is *my* favourite place to get *my* favourite treat. She actually ate one too. Maple glazed – my recommendation. I tried not to notice that the doughnuts place is in the opposite direction to Tasha's house. Tasha said she'd just go home. She looked kind of dejected as she peeled off from us. I'm hoping it was just because she wanted a chocolate cream puff.

At school, Aimee is waiting for me outside our form room.

"Your hair always looks so cool!" she says. I'm wearing a standard topknot but yeah, I guess my curls are kind of impressive, even tied back.

Our first period is the one lesson we're actually in together. It's Spanish with Sr Mustard (I kid you not) and we're both kind of useless at it. Usually, Aimee sits on the other side of Tasha and I can't hear anything they're saying but today, without having to ask her, Tasha is suddenly relegated to the other side and Aimee is next to me. Aimee talks to me the whole lesson. Making little jokes. Asking for my help or helping me out. Pairing up with me for conversation. I know she's a bit of an actress. The thing is, she's good. It's actually really fun to be on her good side. She's genuinely hilarious. My tummy hurts from laughing so much at break time when we share a bag of chocolate buttons. Yeah, OK, sometimes the jokes are at the expense of other people, but she's not saying it *to* them. She's just saying it to me and she's kind of good at picking up on people's little quirks. I hadn't even really noticed that Tony Jones had sleepy eyes, or Amber Allen wore baby shoes. She slays me with an impression of Michael Cotton trying to say he has forgotten his book in Spanish. I don't even know why it is so funny, but I can hardly breathe.

She's messaging me privately over dinner. She's asking if I have plans this weekend and do I want to go and get a manicure at her cousin's salon and then go to the cinema. That definitely sounds like more fun than what I was going to do— homework and the Hollyoaks omnibus. She says Sebastian and his friends are going to the cinema too. Whatever. The film sounds fun and I've never had my nails done professionally. Sounds sort of awesome.

I'm in such a good mood I even accept Dad's offer of a quick workout in his garage gym. He's really surprised. He plays one of his workout playlists, it's called BOUNCE, but I know it used to be called HENRY. Henry was Dad's boyfriend for two years.

"I really like this playlist, Dad," I say. "You haven't played it for a while."

"I know, I've missed these songs!" he says, jumping double time over a skipping rope.

"Do you miss him?" I say, concentrating my eyes on a spot on the wall while I do star jumps.

"Sometimes. But it's OK. These songs still make me happy." He hands me the rope and switches to squat jumps.

"It's OK if you want to bring home someone new, sometime?" I manage to say between jumps over the rope.

"The chance to take the Lena test is a great privilege. No one recently has been worthy of such an honour." He laughs and hits the stopwatch.

Aimee: Where you at?
Was doing a workout with my dad!
Hardcore. Wish I was as fit as you!

ALICE

Caro and Jodie want me to come for a sleepover on Friday and I'm trying to work out if I could get my run in beforehand. I don't want to miss a session but because my running week starts on Saturday, I'll run out of days if I don't run Friday. I can't go tonight because my Aunt Juliet is coming over and everyone really will be suspicious if I volunteer to take Philip out while she's round. Or she'll want to come too. She loves Philip. He's less keen on her because she has a miniature daschund called Kebab and you can see in Philip's eyes he just thinks, *seriously, what is the point of a small dog?* I secretly agree, but I suppose Kebab looks pretty cute in the little bow ties Juliet puts on his collar. I'd never degrade Philip with any human clothes.

Anyway, I need to get run number three done on Friday

so my new week can start on Saturday. Sarah and I are really making progress now. I ran for a full minute and not only did I not die, I did it again a few minutes later. I still don't actually enjoy the feeling when I'm doing it – it still hurts – but I *really* enjoy the feeling afterwards. I am super smug smugly smuggerson, and I go home and put my jimjams on and then I'm snug snuggly snuggerson. Sometimes I skip the rest days if I get the opportunity but this week has been really difficult because my dad has taken Philip out himself several times. Without being asked. The pest! It's not that Philip would object to two walks in one night, I'm just not ready to tell anyone about my best friend Sarah and our secret running club yet. Not my family and *definitely* not my actual best friends. Hm. Let's not dwell on that. DOORBELL!

Juliet arrives with Kebab and what I thought was an actual kebab but it turns out it's a huge portion of chips (from the kebab shop). She claims Mum never makes enough food. Mum always makes enough food. It's just that the food is salad and rice and vegetables. Mum is a vegan. Dad is a vegetarian. Clara and I are sort of pescatarian at home (can't resist Captain Birdseye – also can't resist a burger when I'm out) and Juliet is just some sort of fast-food junkie posing as a trendy clean-eating health freak. She eats more brownies than anyone I know. Some of them are made with raw cacao and sweet potato and are disgusting, but most of them are just made with butter and chocolate. She eyes me up and down when she sees me and I can tell she's seeing something different in me.

"You're taller," she finally says.

"No, you're taller!" I say, standing next to her. We're an exceedingly tall family, for sure, but Juliet's an absolute skyscraper. She's like mum; yoga-slender and graceful with it. I get my bulk from Dad who is tall *and* broad. Lucky me.

"I luuuuurve your trainers!" Juliet is wearing some sort of golden chariots on her feet. They're actually gold and the leather is all patterned like lace. The soles look super cushioned and bouncy too. I need to get some decent trainers.

"Can I try them on?"

They're too big for me but they are so beautiful I take a photo of them anyway and upload it #DearSanta.

"I love your leggings and sweater too." I can't help but lust over Juliet's swanky gym gear, but there's nothing new about that. I used to want her clothes to wear to non-uniform days at school. Now I want them to actually do sports in! Who'd have thought it?

"Er, Juliet. These soles are still pristine. Do you actually wear these to run in?"

"Well, I haven't yet, but I might do twenty minutes on the running machines before my pilates class."

"But, don't you ever run outside?"

"Nah," she says, as she chomps a chip. "Ruins your shoes."

OK, now this is dedication. I've decided to go to Caro's tonight AND do my run, which is why I'm walking Philip at six o'clock in the chuffing morning. And I am chuffing, because we've skipped the whole warm-up walk and gone straight into the running – and we're not even near the posh houses yet. There wasn't time to wait for 'Scruples' to come into view. If it wasn't ridiculous a.m. I'd be more worried about seeing someone I know but honestly, who else is going to be out at this time beyond other mad runners and dog walkers. Minnie Michaels had better appreciate this.

I've left a note for Mum and/or Dad saying I couldn't sleep so I came down for breakfast but then Philip pestered me for a walk. It was quite a long note. I added details for authenticity but thinking back it looks more like I've written the beginning of a really rubbish novel. Anyway, we're here now and we'll deal with the consequences when I get back. With any luck it'll be before anyone is awake and I can throw my creative writing in the bin.

Sarah says I'm doing so well. We're going to be really stretching out the running soon and it's going to be totally fine. Today we're doing some ninety-seconds running and walking and then some three-minute runs and three-minute walks. If you'd told me a few weeks ago I'd be able to run for three minutes without stopping I'd have said . . . well, I would have said that sounds like a piece of cake, I can do that any day of the week. But I'd have been wrong. I didn't know how awful and difficult running was back then, in my youth.

In a mere six weeks or less I'll be able to run for thirty minutes without stopping and that, my friend, is an acceptable distance to say you're going out for 'A Run'. Maybe that's when I'll feel like it's OK to say it to my mum and dad, and maybe even Jodie and Caro. And then I'll be able to ask Mum for some golden chariot trainers and sweat-wicking t-shirts.

I'd feel a lot more confident about all that if I wasn't finding this last three minutes to be an absolute beast.

How on earth am I going to run these three minutes ten times over? Oh shut up, Alice. We'll deal with that final week monstrosity when we come to it. Trust in the podcast. Trust in Sarah. She's never let me down before. She's always got some wise words to spur me on. Speak to me Sarah . . .

. . . Sarah?

"Just two more minutes to go!"

I've never liked you, Sarah.

MINNIE

We're hiding out at my house. Daniel doesn't know we're hiding. He thinks we're just crashing out in front of the TV because that's what couples usually do. It's not what we usually do, but since my accident all sorts of things are not usual.

Now I'm a person who doesn't have practice to go to, or a match to prepare for. Now I'm a person who won't join the county team. Now I'm a person who won't make the Superleague. Now I'm a person who binges TV series and eats a whole tub of Pringles without realising it.

My phone is flashing at me but I'm not even going to look at it.

Seeing all the team's group chats and not really being part of them has made it all seem sort of . . . boring. They don't really talk about anything real. It's just pep talks and woo-hoos and lolz and remembering things that only just happened. I feel like I suddenly don't know these girls. How have I never noticed that I don't know when Sophie's birthday is. Or if Bella has any brothers or sisters. I definitely don't know if any of them have hopes and dreams beyond netball. Other hobbies, perhaps. Oh god, what if they all have other things they do. Maybe Tina B is an amazing chef. Maybe Naomi can play the piano. For all I know, Emily is planning to study Astrophysics at university and Melanie is a keen historian. Whoever they are, they don't want me killing the mood with my horrible BurgerShack experience, but I do want to talk to someone.

Daniel has fallen asleep. He looks so comfortable. Isn't he always?

I take a breath, and message Sophie privately.

Hey, do you want to grab a coffee this weekend?

She replies instantly. Hey, I would have loved that but I have my weekend job.xx

Sophie has a job! I didn't know that. I've never even thought about getting a job.

I spend the next forty-five minutes stirring myself into another horrible mood. Thinking about Sophie and her job. The other girls and their busy lives. I think about the girls at BurgerShack, laughing at my hair. Laughing at me. And for some reason, I think about standing for those photos, pretending to laugh with Lena and Alice Daly-Donne. We laughed like we had shared the best joke ever, but it wasn't real. The end credits music wakes Daniel up and he smiles at me with sleepy eyes.

"What did I miss?" he says.

I can't be bothered to tell him what happened in the episode. It was stupid and I wasn't really following it.

"I don't know," I say.

"What do you mean you don't know? Did you fall asleep too? I can rewind it." He's confused and I can't bring myself to help him.

"No. I didn't sleep!" I say it louder than I mean to. Angrier too. He's really confused now.

"Um, OK?"

"I don't want to watch it again!" The idea of sitting through it again is making my stomach churn.

"Right . . ." he switches the TV off and stands up. "Is there something wrong?"

"I'm just . . ." I have no idea what I am just. ". . .

tired. Uncomfortable on the sofa. I want to go to bed."
I think this sounds plausible.

". . . Yeah, OK, sure." He's rubbing his head like a bear.
He's so lovely and I'm momentarily even annoyed about
that. Why is he so lovely to me?

I'm just stewing and even though this is totally unlike
me, he doesn't press it.

"All right. See you, then." He lets himself out without
another word.

The text message comes a few minutes after the front
door clicks.

Daniel: Love you, girl.

I can barely see the letters through my tears.

LENA

Aimee has definitely 'forgiven me' about the whole Seb
thing and maybe things are looking up for her with him.
I see them chatting on the side of the field during athletics.
Aimee is waiting for me to finish so we can hang out after
and it looks like he's stayed to keep her company. She is
glowing under his gaze.

I do really well at practice again. I run into the space,
I run through the finish line. I'm ready to do the drill
again and again. I think about Minnie Michaels – when

she's recovered and she comes back to training, I'll be ready for her. She won't know what's happening. I bet she expects to stay on top, even after months out of practice. She'll just show up and expect to be the best because that's the way it's always been. But things are changing. I'm changing.

I wave to Aimee as I get ready to charge off the starting line again.

"Woohooooo, fast as lightning!!" she cries as I burst off the line – yeah, like lightning. White hot. I imagine Minnie running in the lane next to me. Fading back as I strike forward. Crossing the line and waiting for her to catch up. Winning.

Amazingly, Aimee invites me to her house after practice; she's still buzzing about Seb staying to chat to her. We never really spend much time at her house. She always preferred to come to mine. She doesn't ask me to stay for dinner and I wonder what she'll have. I should invite her to my house again sometime, for some of Dad's jerk chicken. Would she even eat it, though?

We sit in her room and I stare at the photo of us she has in a frame on her desk. It's only from her last birthday and it isn't a particular favourite of mine.

She's all glammed up but I thought it was just a sleepover so I'm in my sloppiest sweats. We have our arms around each other but neither of us are really smiling. She's doing a sort of pouty face, the type she does in all her selfies. I'm pretty sure she's only framed this picture because she likes how she looks in it.

Her sisters wander in and out of our conversation. They tease her like, I guess, big sisters do. I wouldn't know. Aimee is pretty harsh back to them.

She talks and talks about Sebastian. "So, do you think he likes me?"

I have no idea. "Yeah, course he does."

"Yeah, he was chatting to me for ages when we were watching you at practice. I don't see why else he would have hung around after school like that."

"Definitely."

"Don't say anything, but I think Tasha is a bit deluded about Max though. I don't think he even knows her name."

"Aw, well, he probably does. I think they have geography together."

"Yeah, well, Lewis definitely likes you."

This is absolute rubbish. Lewis has said about five words to me in person in four years of school. He's never shown the slightest bit of interest in me. But I can see this doesn't matter at all to Aimee. She thinks this is a kindness. A validation of some sort. Hooray, you're fanciable! Is that something I should want? Is that the kind of thing that is important? It is to Aimee. I guess it's like winning a race for her. Getting Sebastian Edwards is beating Minnie Michaels in the 100m.

I don't know why she's got it in for Minnie Michaels too, but it's one thing on her slam list I'm happy to indulge.

"So, did you hear that Minnie Michaels won't be able to play any sports for the rest of the term . . ."

"Not sat on such a high horse now, is she?"

"No horse at all. You can't go riding with a broken neck."

"Shoulder, arm, whatever. I wonder if her arm has withered while it's been recovering."

"My cousin's leg did that! When the cast came off one leg was totally skinny and hairy and so white it was blue."

"Sounds disgusting."

"And just in time for the summer ball . . . shame!"

"Hey, we should go to the ball all together, with Tasha and Nikki. We could all get ready together."

"Oh, but I'll be going with Sebastian and you'll be going with Lewis."

Hmm, we'll see about that. And then she adds, almost to herself. "Ha, yeah and Daniel Turner won't be smug with lop-sided skinny Minnie on his arm."

She's staring at herself in the mirror now. Holding her hair up in various styles. Her eyes almost glazed over and I feel sorry for her. She acts all confident at school but she's filled with so much anger. It seems so misplaced.

"Aimee, are you OK?" I have to try. There was a time we used to talk properly. When we had matching lunchboxes. Before boys were anything more than pests on the playground. Before anyone had a proper haircut she could criticize, or wore mascara that could go clumpy. Come on, Aimee, show me you remember how to be my friend, for real.

"Yeah, course I am – I can't wait for Seb to see me in my dress. We're going to be the main event. God knows what Nikki is going to wear with her figure. Me and you are going to look so fit, though . . ."

ALICE

Jacob Porter is making this art lesson highly amusing and I'm wondering why we don't hang out more. Why isn't it his house I'm going to tonight for a sleepover?

Oh, right yeah, because boys and girls can't be friends without everyone wit-wooing and ooh-la-la-ing. Trust me, there is definitely nothing to wit-woo about me and Jacob Porter. For a start, I think he likes boys and I'm a girl. And not that I'm sizeist or anything, other than to myself, but Jacob Porter is tiny. Like a pixie. The idea of anything romantic occurring between us is not just laughable, it's slapstick. Still, I don't think Mum and Dad would let me sleep over at a boy's house even if he was a gay pixie.

Jacob is telling me some story about trying to follow a contouring tutorial on YouTube and I'm nearly hyperventilating at his descriptions of blending the 'sunbeam' highlighter into the 'tropical blush' to create a sculpted cheekbone ("sculpted like an actual terracotta clay sculpture . . . of a slice of bacon") when Miss Hallam gives us that warning cough to simmer down before she actually has to bother getting up and coming over. I spin around on my chair to try and calm my breathing down and catch sight of Other Jacob's profile. He's bent down towards his sketchbook, so close his eyes must be crossed. His back will be knackered when he stands up. His floppy hair has flopped forward and it's bouncing sensually along with his frantic shading. Is he just colouring the whole page black again? What a weirdo. Did I say sensually? I meant . . . normally. Like with no other feelings about it. Except that he's weird.

And sexy.

I'm staring at him and he's noticed. Of course he has. My eyes are burning holes into his body. I expect him to say 'ouch' or look a bit annoyed but he smiles and tucks his hair back off his face and goes back to his drawing/colouring.

"So, Jacob Altman, is it?"

"No! What? You're my only Jacob!" I say to Jacob Porter, who has a smug little smile on his pesky pixie face.

"Mmmhmm . . ." He's on to me.

"So, tell me more about your bacon creation. How did it turn out in the end?"

He's easily distracted. "HA! It ended up so bad I edited my video – I'd filmed it of course, thought I could be a YouTuber doing amazing make-ups, etc.—"

"Wait, a video of you copying another video?"

"Yeah, babes, it's meta . . ."

"Right."

"So, the video was so funny that I edited it together anyway and called it, 'HELP ME, KIM KARDASHIAN' and it's practically gone viral."

MINNIE

I managed to get nearly three whole weeks off school but as of tomorrow I've got no more excuses. I still wear the sling but my shoulder doesn't hurt any more and sitting on my sofa healing is apparently no different to sitting in a classroom healing while I learn about quadratic equations. So, I've got to go back.

Mum keeps saying, "You'll be excited to get back and see your friends". She blames my horrible new mood on being "cooped up in here for too long". But being cooped up is the only thing keeping me safe from all the faces that I don't want to see. The teams, expecting me to sit on the sidelines and be team-spirit happy until I'm fit enough to play again. The club coach, expecting me to work extra hard to get back up to speed and make those county trials next season. Aimee Bradbury and Lena Singleton . . . I don't know what they're expecting from me, but it feels like the wolves will be waiting for me at the school gates.

My own face is the one I really can't stand because it looks just the same.

How can I explain to myself that something has changed on the inside and I don't want to be that person any more? I don't want to be the person Lena and Aimee were laughing at either. But this isn't about hair. I feel like I've spent the last three weeks unravelling myself and there's nothing solid in the centre. Sport was just something other people told me I should do. Netball and the team and school were just circling around me and all that kept them going was momentum. Netball wasn't so much my identity as a cover for the fact I don't really have one without it. How lame is that?

It turns out, I don't even know what else I like. I know I like Daniel. I know I like being outdoors. I know I like moving. Maybe I like French films? Maybe I can like espresso over vanilla ice cream. I'm trying to write a mental CV for the rest of my life. What are my strengths? I'm struggling to think!

All this, and at the same time I realise I don't even have proper friends to talk to . . .

LENA

I tried again with Aimee at school. I tried to cut her off when she got spiky. I tried to change the subject when she spiralled into a mean girl. Nikki and Tasha never stand up to her but somehow, she twisted my efforts into another Us vs. Them. I don't understand why we can't just all be friends together – why someone has to be the one on the back foot. I even pulled her close and whispered, "you can tell me if something is wrong".

She shoved me away and laughed over my head, calling out to Seb as he passed – "Help! I think she fancies me . . ."

For goodness' sake. She linked her arm through mine and said horrible things about people she didn't even know and I just had to stop listening. I tuned her out and thought about running away.

"You're coming to the park tonight." She wasn't asking.

"No." I needed an excuse she couldn't crash. "I've got running club with my Dad."

God, this is going to make his day. Tonight, I'm finally saying yes. Show me the light, Dad. Pass me that armband. Let's do it. For real. I'm in. I will come to your running club. He invites me every week and I usually say 'homework'. But the truth is, it's late and I'm tired and sometimes I don't want to run in front of him any more than I have to. But tonight, I'm saying yes. He looks surprised. And then he looks really, really happy.

"Mr Day told me you've been smashing it at athletics club."

"Yeah, I've been feeling good."

"That's great, honey. He said you might get picked for the 100m in competition?"

"Wow, really?"

"If you keep running the way you're running!"

His running club is all adults but Dad's been trying to encourage a younger membership for ages. He's always desperate for me to "tell my friends". Ha! Sometimes they meet at the track to practise sprints and things, like Dad and I do on Wednesday mornings. Some nights they go for a long run. The odd night I've attended it's always been at the track so it throws me a little when Dad says we're heading out for a 10K tonight. I've never run that far before. I don't even know if I can.

"Don't worry, Lena. Just do what you can. Make your own pace," he says to me before addressing the group with the route. He has it printed out on a little map and highlighted in blue.

The groups naturally divide into smaller packs as we set off and I run alongside Dad to begin with.

"If you need to slow it down or duck out early, that's fine. I'll see you back at home." I feel relieved he isn't expecting great things from me tonight.

"We'll have pancakes," he adds with a smile.

"Now that's worth running for!" I laugh. And then we don't speak any more. We run side by side and somehow,

I keep pace with him. Some of the really fast runners are already out of sight in front of us and there's a group we've lost way behind too. A few pairs and single runners are dotted around us. All I can hear is the sound of running feet and our breath in the cool evening air.

After twenty minutes or so Dad says, "How are you doing?"

I'm surprised to hear myself say, "I'm great. I'm loving it! . . . You're a good coach, Dad."

He smiles and we keep running.

"I AM RUNNING!" he calls out to the group.

"WE ARE RUNNING!" they reply. And we just keep going.

Unbelievably, I complete the route. I get tired towards the end and I think Dad has slowed his pace right down to stay with me. Some of the others have overtaken us in the last ten minutes but we're there. At the end of the blue line.

"My first 10K!" I say, between deep lungfuls of breath. I'm suddenly exhausted.

"My girl!" Dad says. "A natural-born long-distance runner. That was beautiful."

I think it kind of was.

ALICE

OK, so our sleepovers are really fun. We get loads of food. Caro's mum even splashes out on lots of bits from Marks and Spencer including some outrageous lemon and lime jaffa cakes, of which I may have eaten about twelve. We put our pyjamas on and do face masks because that's what happens on sleepovers on TV. None of us ever use face masks at any other time but it's funny because Jodie always accidentally on purpose licks them and then tries to convince us that they actually taste sort of nice. We watch films we have seen a thousand times. *13 Going on 30* is one of our favourites. I think because we all actually do love the idea of being thirty. Working in an office. Wearing smart clothes. Stapling things. Drinking coffee out of cardboard cups.

Of course, we spend a lot of time scrolling.

"You haven't been posting very much," Caro says.

"Um, I guess I haven't been doing anything."

"That's never stopped you before."

Fair. "I'll do one now. I've tagged you both." It's a picture of a jaffa cake.

I get four likes almost instantly. Caro and Jodie, naturally. Jacob Porter and Other Jacob! Is he a fan of jaffa cakes? Well, to be honest, who isn't? But also, he has never liked any of my posts before. I have a rummage around his profile. He barely uses it. This is a very exciting development. I will have to try a few more posts over the next few days. If he likes them all, he's in love with me. If he doesn't, he just really likes jaffa cakes.

The rest of the night is a blur of Cajun-spiced pitta chips and Moroccan hummus mixed with a bit of YouTube-oke (it's like karaoke but you just sing/shout over the song and no one knows the right words). I don't know why I was nervous about this. They're my best friends. They still have a few giggles about some things I don't know about, but whatever.

We talk about the summer ball and how we're all going to wear fifties-style dresses like we're in *Grease*. I suggest it might be funnier to dress like we're *in* our fifties and raid our Mums' wardrobes.

Jodie says there's a shop in town that specialises in vintage-style dresses and they have loads of good ones, and then she says to me, "You can even wear them with trainers and still look cute."

I don't wear high heels. Never have. I love this idea. I could wear my dress with trainers, and if they're my party shoes they'd need to be a bit more glam than my skanky old Vans.

"I've seen the perfect pair!" I say. I show them Juliet's amazing gold trainers on my phone and they agree they are entirely appropriate for a ball.

"Ball-worthy," Caro says.

"You're ball-worthy!" I reply and we descend into another fit of hyena laughter.

We post a selfie with the caption BALL-WORTHY. Jacob Altman likes it.

MINNIE

Daniel hasn't come to meet me. We never plan to walk in together, he just usually turns up or finds me en route and today he just hasn't. I'm nearly at the gates and I'm wondering if I should just keep on walking.

I couldn't bring myself to apologise for my weird mood because I still can't explain what I'm angry about. He did send me our usual love you message when he left but only because it would have been a *major* statement to withhold that. He was giving me a pass, but now it's my turn to make things better.

I slide into registration and try to avoid eye contact with everyone. I hide my phone under my desk and text him.

I'm sorry. It's me, not you.

He replies a moment later.

I know.

Ouch. I don't know how to respond. He is typing again.

What is *it* though?

I don't know.

I'm lost.

Me too.

MIN, ARE YOU BREAKING UP WITH ME DURING REGISTRATION?

I gasp aloud and a few people turn around to see what I'm up to. Luckily our form tutor is uninterested.

NO!!!!!!!!!!!!!!!!!!!!!!!!!!!!!!!!!!!

Cool. Meet you at break.

LENA

Minnie Michaels came back to school today. I only glimpsed her, and she's still wearing a sling, but her presence triggers a little niggle in my brain. She's coming back to ruin my winning streak. Steal all my good vibes. Show me up in front of my Dad.

I don't want to share the track with her again. The thought of her getting knocked down bursts in my vision like a firework. I could do with her having another accident. I catch my ugly thought and stop myself. No, I'll just have to beat her.

Aimee's face looks how I feel. But her anger goes off in weird directions.

"So, his beloved remembered to wash her hair today. What does he even see in her? He must be thicker than he looks." It changes direction and hurtles towards Nikki. "What do you think, NikNak? Do you think he could do better than her?"

Nikki gives it a go. "Yeah, definitely. You're way prettier than her."

Too far.

"I didn't say anything about me! Eugh! As if I'd go near *him*."

"She's still hiding that mouldy arm away," I say, immediately furious for getting involved. I'm trying to take the heat off Nikki but Aimee takes it as an allegiance; I'm on her side. She roars with conspiratorial laughter. I feel sick. The others duly laugh along. She selects a new target.

"What's funny about that, Tasha?"

She stops laughing.

Aimee prepares to fire. "You weren't there when we talked about her mouldy arm. You don't know about that."

Tasha looks for help. Nikki avoids her eyes. Target engaged.

"Aimee's cousin's leg went mouldy inside his cast."
I don't know why I said that.

"Yeah, Tasha . . . are you laughing at my cousin?"

Kaboom!

Tasha is left gawping amongst the rubble of that insane exchange.

Aimee fixes me with a smile, "See you at lunch, Lena. Let's get chips!"

Aimee isn't in my form. I sit with Nikki and Tasha but today they barely speak to me. They barely speak to each other, either. It's like they're holding their breath.

"Did you have good weekends?" I say to break the awkward silence.

"Yeah, thanks," clips Nikki.

"Nothing special," says Tasha.

That's all I'm getting from them.

I can't even think of anything else to say. Minnie Michaels passes our form room on the way to her first lesson.

"I could have done with her never coming back!" I say.

Nikki and Tasha give me a really strange look.

". . . Yeah."

"Totally!"

They offer, like robots. And then I realise why they're being so weird with me.

They're scared.

ALICE

I can't help but look for Other Jacob at break time. We don't have many classes together and I won't officially see him until Physics at fifth period, but for some reason I'm desperate to know he's at school. Just a glimpse now so I know I'll see him later. Ever since I realised he's in love with me (he's liked three posts of mine now) I've been thinking about him non-stop. I've decided I should get to know him, to see if his personality is as handsome as his face/hair combo.

Jodie and Caro are deep in analysis of their Spanish lesson that happened five minutes ago. They can't decide if their teacher, Sr Mustard, is hot or not. I've seen him. He's definitely not. But they just keep shushing me and saying there's "something about him". Aside from the fact he's genuinely called Mr Mustard (outside Español lessons, of course), he honestly wears mustard-coloured cord trousers and he has a blonde waxed moustache that curls up at the edges. Just like Colonel

Mustard! I bet he does Cluedo cosplay at board game conventions. But he's young and clearly a bit of a hipster and he's under forty, so by school decree he has some level of attractiveness, if only in comparison to the rest of the ogres on the staff.

"*Un poco caliente!*" Caro is saying in an OTT accent.

"*Salsa amarillo!*" I offer, because 'yellow sauce' was the closest I could get to mustard on Google translate.

Other Jacob swoops into my view and I hear the theme from *Phantom of the Opera* in my head. That would be Jacob's theme music because he's so dark and brooding, and also because I need to stop comparing him to Snow White. He's drinking some water. He's walking across the playground. He's ... really not doing anything interesting at all. He waves at someone. Australian Daniel. He goes into the Art Hut. That's it. I wonder if he was looking for me. Maybe he was thinking about me as he walked across that playground. Was he wondering if there were any new posts he could like as he drank that water? Probably. Maybe he's not even working on his artwork. He's gone to stalk me online. I stalk him online.

Nothing.

MINNIE

Being back at school is strange. I feel like I've undergone this huge transformation and nobody has noticed. Captain Bella and Sophie are delighted to have me back and "why haven't I been on group chat?" and I missed this thing at practice last night that was "so funny" and when will I "lose the sling" and, more importantly, when can I play for the club again? The truth is, I could take the sling off now; the doctor said I'd made fantastic progress. But I convinced Mum I should wear it to school in case someone knocked into me in the busy corridors. I don't even know why I wanted to keep it on. It's totally annoying, but, for some reason, I'm not ready to look like I can play netball yet . . .

Bella says not to worry about missing the county scouts – "We didn't even win the games they were at" and, anyway, "they will be there again next season . . ."

They gabble at me at 100 miles an hour and don't seem to notice that I don't say much in return. We walk past Aimee Bradbury and Lena Singleton and I'm sure they burst into laughter when I'm on the other side. What is their problem?

Daniel's waiting for me after my first class and we find a bench at break time to sit and talk.

"How do you feel?"

"Kind of weird."

"Your shoulder feels OK?"

"Yeah, it feels fine."

"Good. So, what's weird?"

"I don't know how to explain it, really."

"Just talk then."

"OK, so, in the future, what do you imagine your life to be like?"

Daniel screws up his face a little. Clearly, he wasn't expecting me to say that.

"I don't know, really. I think I'll grow a beard. Or at least some designer stubble."

"Be serious."

"I'll get ripped too. Seriously ripped. You'll wanna stick with me."

I pause. "*Do* you think we'll stick together?"

He doesn't miss a beat.

"Yeah, why not? We're good together."

I give his hand a little squeeze. "I think so, too!"

"So, what's the problem?"

I take a breath. "In this future, with us together, where are we and what are we doing? Like, what is my job? What am I like as a grown-up? What do I like doing?"

He stops to think and I wonder how long it will take for him to realise he has only ever imagined me as I am now. Playing netball. Running sprints. Climbing walls. Riding bikes. Because that's all I am. Minnie Michaels, you know, the *sporty* one. But that's not a thing to be for the rest of your life. And actually, when I think about it – and it's all I have thought about recently – I'm starting to realise that I don't actually *want* that life. I don't want early morning training sessions and competition weekends. I definitely don't want dieticians and personal trainers dictating my day. I don't want a career that suddenly ends when someone else starts beating me. It seems that I know all about what *I don't want*. What I'm not sure about is what *I do want*. And how do I even find out if no one will let me be anything other than sporty?

Daniel wraps his arm around my neck and pulls me in close. "My magic ball sees the future very clearly and in it, like I said, I'm really ripped and you are gorgeous, of course. You are fun to be around, you're kind and thoughtful, you're smart and you're brave. We have a blast."

"But what are we doing?"

"We're doing everything. Living our lives. Living our best lives! The world is our oyster!"

"You're not worried?"

"Not even for a second."

There is nothing wrong with anything he has said. There is everything right with what he has said. I still need a little more, though. I feel embarrassed, but I trust him with everything.

"Daniel, if I don't play netball, what am I going to do? I don't even know what else I like."

"Lucky we're only babies and have a ton of time to find out then." He's smiling, but then he stops and fixes me with a serious look. "Minnie, you don't need to know that yet. We're young. We really are. And people change careers over and over. Even if you get your dream job at twenty-five, it doesn't mean it will be your dream job at thirty-five."

"But you know what you want to do . . ."

"No, I know I want to go to a uni with a great engineering course because that's what I like doing at the moment. I'm only ever looking to my immediate future. Just the next few steps."

"What are my next few steps?"

"You're like Bambi. Just learning to walk again. Your next few steps should be like, finding your feet. Testing the ground. But all sorts of different grounds. To find out what you like, if you want to give the netball thing a break for a while."

He's too cute to be this wise. I wonder if he realises that I don't have other friends I can talk to like this. That he's my everything. And perhaps that's not the way it should be.

"BUT – you could still play netball if you wanted. Your injury hasn't changed that."

"I know," I say, actually hearing myself, "but it's changed me."

ATTENTION!

Time is running out to apply for the
Tricolore Exchange Summer Programme.
Application forms can be
collected from the school office
and must be signed by your
languages teacher AND
form tutor before sending.

Don't miss this fantastic
opportunity to visit Paris
and improve your French.

À bientôt!

PART FOUR: SPRINT!

LENA

It's athletics after school and even though she's not running, everyone's talking about the return of Minnie Michaels. When will she be back to athletics club? Will she have lost any of her speed?

"Will she be able to beat Lena cos she has been *fast* these last few weeks." I heard that last comment in the changing rooms. It made my heart buzz. I'm still feeling creepy about the way Tasha and Nikki were this morning but I'm trying to focus right now. I'm here to run.

Aimee is watching from the edge of the field. I never ask her to wait but she's taken it upon herself to come to every practice now. She thinks she'll bump into Seb again.

Half of me hates the idea of lining up alongside Minnie on this start line again. Half of me can't wait to beat her.

Ready, set, go!

I fire away from the start. Arms pumping. Picking my feet up. Clean strikes. Knees high. Fast, fast, faster. I see the finish line ahead. It always amazes me how much time I have to think in such a short distance. When I do those sprints with my dad, I think about how much I hate it. Now I think about her. Do I make it look as easy as she used to? Now that I'm winning? And suddenly I'm at the finish line.

But I haven't won.

A girl with red hair has come out of nowhere and beaten me. She wasn't even a contender. Where has she been hiding that speed?

We go again and I line up ready. I can't have concentrated properly the first time. I was distracted.

Ready, set, go!

Push. Focus. Run.

I come in third. This is unbelievable. Some girl from the year below takes the win this time. Redhead comes second.

We line up for the 200m. I feel like I run really well. My technique is good. I give it everything I've got. But I don't win once. A girl that I think is called Tanya wins the race by a mile. How have I never noticed these other runners before? Have they always been this good or am I just having a really, really, bad day?

We finish practice and I'm in a rage. I storm off the track and Aimee jumps into my eyeline.

"That gingernut girl needs a spray tan, stat! Let's go get milkshakes. Maybe Seb and Lewis are at BurgerShack."

She doesn't get that I'm upset about this. "No, thanks," I say.

"What?" Aimee looks totally unimpressed.

"I don't want to go. Sorry." But I'm not sorry. I don't need to apologise for that. We didn't have plans. I just want to go home. So I do. I turn away from her and start to run.

"Lena! What the hell!?" Aimee shouts after me. I keep running. And when I get home, I realise I don't want to stop there either. I throw my bag in the door and head straight back out.

I run down to the beach and along the promenade. I run around the golf course and I keep running. I can't work out what I'm feeling. I thought I was embarrassed that I didn't win those sprints, but some part of me knows that isn't really it. I pass churches and schools and I can't stop. I run past other runners who smile and nod at me. I keep running and I find that the knot of anger begins to loosen. I run past dog walkers and pairs of mums pushing prams. I feel the truth start to unfurl with each stride. I run some more until it's right in front of me; I don't like who I am when I'm with Aimee. I don't like the way she talks about other people. I don't like the way I feel pressured to take part and then say things I don't even mean. I don't like the way I feel nervous about being on the receiving end. I run past an old couple on a bench eating ice cream cones. The lady waves at me. I keep running. I don't like the way we aren't honest with each other. I don't like the way we don't actually have fun. I don't like the way we do have fun when it's at the expense of other people. I don't like the way I find myself literally running away from her rather than telling her how I feel. I don't like that I don't love my best friend anymore. I run past the boating lake and down the cycle path. I turn into the wooded area where it's cool and dark. I run across leaves and my feet sound different. I run past a small dog carrying a massive stick. I feel lighter. Even just acknowledging the truth feels good. It's time to make a change. I keep running until I feel myself actually smiling. Running and breathing and smiling. I run past a little boy on a scooter who scoots alongside me until his dad calls him back. I run past a man that my dad trains and then I run past someone from the local running club who recognises me. He's running in the opposite direction and we beam at each other. As he passes he says, "Good work, Lena!"

I take a turn down an alley I've never been down before. I think it comes out near my road. Another runner is approaching me. It takes a while to focus my eyes but as we cross, I recognise her. It's Big Alice! Sorry, it's just Alice. She's breathing hard but she looks so focused. There wasn't time to smile or say hello. I look back over my shoulder but she isn't looking over hers. I didn't know she was a runner. I check my watch. I've been running for over an hour.

I get home and take a shower. I find myself still smiling in the bathroom mirror. My cheeks are warm to the touch. I feel like I really worked something out. I feel like I really let myself be heard. I think I finally understand what Dad means when he says running is as "good for the soul as it is for the body".

ALICE

Sarah really drops a bombshell on me tonight. She's tricked me by changing up the plan within the same week. The first two sessions this week have been our usual walk run walky run walky walky run run with the run time creeping up and the walking time creeping down like I wouldn't notice. I did notice, Sarah, but I also did complete it, so thank you for getting me through that. So tonight, I was expecting more of the same and she hits me right in the earhole with a twenty-minute run!! What the hell, Sarah?!

She breaks the news to me while we're on our brisk five-minute warm-up walk and it almost floors me. I start imagining a pain in my stomach. I start apologising to Sarah for having to go home because of this awful headache, or tummy ache, or whatever it was. I vow to do the session another night, when I'm feeling better, and I'm about to turn around when she says, "go" and starts the funky running music – and I automatically start running.

There's a lot of panting and a lot of sweating and maybe a little bit of swearing. At some point I see flashes in the corner of my eyes and I can't tell if I've been papped again or I'm having a stroke. But somehow, some way, I run for the whole twenty minutes. I don't even stop when I cross paths with my silent fake friend from school, even though I sort of die on the spot with embarrassment. Lena is running faster than me so we pass quickly; there isn't enough time to fully melt into the ground, so I just keep my head down and power on. Sarah needs me to complete this run and I don't want to let her down.

Of course, Lena Singleton *would* be out for a run. She probably does a marathon after school every night. Everyone knows she's a runner, but no one knows that I am an attempted runner. Except now she does. Oh, god. The cringe factor shoots way beyond the time I had to keep running past the old people's home and they all stood at the window and clapped. She'll know and tell everyone she saw me huffing and puffing away in my Tesco leggings and my mum's trainers. Don't ask me how she'll know about those things. She will.

Worrying about having Tesco branded across my bum actually gets me through minutes eighteen and nineteen, and when Sarah says I've got just sixty seconds left I forget about Lena and concentrate on enjoying this. I'm about to complete a twenty-minute run! I'm actually going to do it! And if I can do twenty, there's no reason I can't do twenty-five. And thirty. Sarah will get me there. I should never have doubted you, Sarah. I'm sorry, you are brilliant.

Sarah counts down the last ten seconds and I give a little "woohoo". I did it!

But I've misjudged where to turn around and now there is a long way to walk home, even after the cool-down minutes. I walk the rest of the way alone with my thoughts. My thoughts are mostly "I am awesome".

While I'm glowing with pride, with rose-tinted cheeks and all-natural luminescent highlighter (a.k.a. sweat), I snap a selfie and send it to Jacob Porter.

I think I've contoured with perspiration

LMAO, you can be in my next video

Actually, I'm thinking of making my own vlogs — "Help me, Mo Farah!" I send it without realising this could expose me as an attempted runner.

I would totally be your first subscriber.

I glide back through the door and Clara is waiting for me at the bottom of the stairs.

"Hello, baby sister. Are you waiting for me?"

"Yes. Can I have a biscuit?"

"Let's both have one."

Clara and I are munching on custard creams and drinking glasses of chocolate milk when Mum comes into the kitchen.

"Good run, darling?"

"Actually, Mum, it was my best yet. Wait. What?"

"Good, well done you. I'm really proud of you."

". . . for what?"

"For taking it upon yourself to get fit. I wish I had your determination!"

"But you don't know about that. That's my secret."

"Oh, but I do know."

"How long have you known for?"

"Since you started 'taking Philip out', but didn't actually take Philip with you any more."

Oh yeah. Clara steals the half-eaten biscuit from my hand. It's poised somewhere between my mouth and the table because I'm frozen in shock.

"Hello, girls!" Dad comes into the kitchen and takes a slurp of my chocolate milk. "Good run, Alice?"

MINNIE

Right, so, I made a little to-do list in my head of things that I think will help me sort my life out. I'm not telling Daniel, but right at the top of the list is to make a friend outside of the team. I know Captain Bella is a fun person to be around and I could see myself hanging out with Sophie, but I think to actually help myself I need to look beyond the netball court. I know Daniel doesn't mind coming shopping with me for a dress for the ball but it'd be more fun if I had a friend to go and try dresses on with, so I could surprise him with mine on the night. We could get our hair done together and paint each other's nails – I'd better start growing them. Maybe my new friend would take me to some shop I've never been to before or we'd go for coffee after shopping and she'd let me try her hazelnut latte. I've never ordered one of those because what if it's not as good as hot chocolate?

God, is it any wonder I got into this mess when I can't even risk a different drink?! New entry on the to-do list is to order a hazelnut latte.

And there's no time like the present.

I'm sitting in the shopping mall's coffee shop with a steaming hazelnut latte and feeling a bit weird because I'm here on my own. I grabbed a fiver from my secret stash of emergency money and just ran out the door. It's only now I'm sat here I've realised I left my phone plugged in charging so I can't text Daniel or read back our old messages, which is something I do when I'm waiting for him sometimes. Sad, isn't it? My coffee still looks too hot to drink. I look around for something to do with my hands and thankfully there are a few discarded magazines on the next empty table. I peel one off the stack and have a flick through. Nice dresses. Shoes that are too high for anyone to wear on a normal day. Make-up that looks too glamorous for anything other than being a model in a fashion magazine, or so I think until I realise the girl who made my latte is wearing the same bold lip colour, like a deep velvety plum. She's got really lovely clear skin which she's kept make-up free, but her eyelids have a shiny iridescent sparkle to them. She looks amazing, and here she is, rocking the same look as the magazine girl, on a wet after-school Thursday. I check the mirror behind me to find my own face. I look about twelve. Ponytail, as usual. Make-up free. Jewellery free. No distinguishing marks of any kind. I know I'm not ugly. I know I'm even sort of pretty. Could I get away with a plum lipstick? Maybe not, but maybe I could try the sparkly eyes? When I've finished my coffee, I'll have a look in Boots.

I read an article about a woman who gave up her job as a lawyer to make baby clothes. One of her designs was shown on a celebrity's social media and her sales rocketed and now she's opening her first store in Brighton. She's changed her life at fifty-two. Daniel was right – nothing needs to be set in stone. I can try things out. Try things on.

I try my coffee. It tastes like a warm Nutella milkshake. Less sophisticated than I imagined, but definitely delicious.

Hazelnut lattes can be my new drink, I think to myself, planning all the times I'm going to come here on my own and read magazines about inspirational women and drink hazelnut lattes – and then I think no, because next time I will try the almond macchiato.

I add some more things to my to-do list.

TO-DO LIST

1. Stop reading old messages instead of actually reading. So, carry a book or a magazine in my bag.
2. Go and buy a book or a magazine to keep in my bag.
3. Look into joining a club outside of school as a way of meeting new people.
4. Make an actual friend.
5. Try and look a bit more grown-up. Try some make-up or a different hair style?
6. Watch another French film.
7. Order the espresso and vanilla ice cream
   7.a. in France??!!??

LENA

I'm watching Alice eat a slice of carrot cake and wondering why I've never really noticed her before. Sure, I was aware she existed; everyone knows of 'Big Alice'. But now I'm *really* looking at her. She's laughing with her friends. She looks totally . . . at ease. Enjoying the cake. Enjoying her friends. She looks like she doesn't have any weight on her shoulders.

Aimee slumps down next to me and sees me looking.

"She should not be adding cake to those thunder thighs!" she says. I hear her and it shocks me. Out-and-out cruel. I can't bring myself to look at her in case I accidentally agree. I bet Alice would never say anything spiteful like that. I know Minnie Michaels never would. How did I end up with such a raw deal in the friendship stakes? I feel like I want to jump up and run away. Leap over the table, push my lunch on to Aimee's lap. Run out of the school gates and down the road. I want to run and run and run.

Alice runs. Maybe that's why she's so happy and relaxed. She probably runs every night after school. Maybe she runs a long one at the weekends. Early on a Sunday morning when there's no one else about. Maybe she gets home after school and changes straight into her gear and goes flying out the door, leaving all her troubles behind her. She goes to bed tired and happy. How I felt last night, but without the dread of the next day because she knows the secret. Take it all in and then run it all out. Take whatever school has to throw at you and then run it all away. That's the answer. Well, that and not having a best friend you secretly want rid of.

"Am I right?!" Aimee is still talking to me. I haven't heard a word.

"Leee-Naaaa! Hell-o-oo! Wakey wakey!"

"What?" I snap.

I see her quash a flash of anger. I see her decide to keep it sweet.

"I was just saying we should go dress shopping for the ball this weekend!"

"Oh right." I do *not* want to do that. "Wait, aren't we going to your cousin's salon to get manicures though?" I was actually quite looking forward to that.

"Oh, yeah, well she's fully booked this weekend. I'll make sure she sees us before the ball though. She'll do it for free and she's totally brilliant at it, you can have any type you want. She worked in London and did all the celebrities!"

"Wow, OK, great." Can't argue with that.

Aimee continues to talk near me about things we are

going to do together. Or rather, things she wants to do that I have been granted permission to bear witness to. I'm really starting to resent being the chosen one. Nikki never comes to the cafeteria with me any more, not since Aimee started. She still doesn't eat anything, but she goes through this pathetic parade every time.

"I'm starving." "Oooh! Pizza! Or chips? Or both?!" then orders a Diet Coke and claims to have had a big breakfast or eaten three chocolate bars at break. Which of course I know she didn't, because she was talking near me then, too.

I decide there and then that I'm going to go for a run after school. A long one.

Aimee witters on about nothing. I'm staring at Alice again, wondering how I could join her group. Could I just go over there and sit with them and act like it was normal? No, probably not.

Aimee senses my apathy and I can hear the tones in her voice shift from self-absorption through frustration to fake interest.

"So, have you got a session with your dad tonight? Maybe I should come round sometime and do it with you. I really need to tone up . . ."

"No, I'm going for a run tonight."

"Oh . . . so cool. OK, so message me when you get back though, yeah?"

And, without realising I'm doing it, I've stood up and walked away . . .

ALICE

Sarah's been really upfront with me this week. I think she feels bad about tricking me last week. She says we're going to do three twenty-five-minute runs this week. I'm trying not to have any reaction at all to this because I know I completed the twenty minutes last week, but that doesn't mean those extra five minutes today won't be a challenge. And horrific. I also can't let myself think that twenty-five minutes is totally impossible because, well, it's not. So, I'm trying to be casual. Keeping it cas'. Whatever, Sarah. Let's not make a big deal out of it. On my marks. Let's get set. Go, go, go!

We're running. I'm keeping my cool. We've got a long way to go so I've got to concentrate on finding that comfortable pace asap. I feel like the struggling train in *Dumbo* who wheezes, "I think I can, I think I can, I think I can" as it huffs up a hill. I say it aloud as my feet strike the ground. *I. think. I. can. I. think. I. can. I. think. I. can.* That's one motivational locomotive.

We're ten minutes in and honestly, I'm feeling OK. Minnie Michaels would be proud. I've managed to keep my little train pace and it's working for me. I've even managed to think about some other things. Namely Jacob Altman. I think I'm going to strike up a conversation in class tomorrow. What have I got to lose? Even if he only 'likes' me as a friend, it's still OK to talk to that friend, isn't it? This is where online etiquette confuses me a little, all those 'friends' that I really would never speak to at school – do they want me to speak to them? Why don't they speak to me? Did they just follow me so they could spy on my life? My profile is dullsville at the moment. Anyway, Jacob. I'm going to say hi. If he's crippled with shyness then it's up to me to be brave. For the sake of our potential future friendship and/or romantic relations. We've done fifteen minutes! Sarah says I'm doing so brilliantly. She's telling me not to get complacent or overexcited. I've got to keep my pace steady. The next ten minutes could be quite tough. Little does she know I'm the engine that thinks it can. *I. think. I. can. I. think. I. can. I. think. I. can.* I wonder if I should write to the RunTime app people and tell them about the little train. I think that could really help other runners. *I. think. I. can. I know. I. can. I. KNOW. I. CAN. I. KNOW* – eh?

Sarah?

Where are you, Sarah?

I come to an abrupt stop because Sarah has done a runner.
Or rather, I didn't charge my phone. Whichever way you
want to spin it. Either way, she's abandoned me in my
ten minutes of need. Bum. I don't even have a watch on
so I can't just measure the ten minutes myself. Plus, I've
stopped now anyway. *BUM, BUM, BUM!* I'm so annoyed
that I barely notice the other runner heading towards me,
until she stops right next to me and it's Lena Singleton
again, talking to me. I take off my headphones.

"Hey. Are you OK?"

"Bloody battery has run out!" I say, a bit rudely, and
then add, "Hello, sorry, hello, hi." Like an idiot. I wonder
if she's going to tell The Girls about this.

"Oh, man. Hate it when that happens," she says.
She's got a nice rosy running glow. I remember I might
look like a tomato. That's probably how she will describe
me when she relays this hilarious anecdote, but in this
moment, I am genuinely more concerned about finishing
this run.

"Grrragh – I don't know what to do now!" I am
genuinely a bit panicked.

"How do you mean?" She's puzzled, of course. "Don't you like running without music?"

Perfect opportunity for me to go, 'Yeah, music, course, can't run without those beats!' But I'm so miffed I just unleash a truth bomb instead.

"It was my RunTime app coach." Whelp.

"Oh, right. What's that?" Course she has never used it.

"It's a programme where people who can't run learn to run, with someone telling you to stop and go. It's better than it sounds."

"But you can run. I've seen you out running before."

"I'm on week seven of the programme."

"Right. Cool. Congratulations. So how far do you have to go?"

"Well, I was fifteen minutes into my first twenty-five-minute run. And then it stopped. And then I stopped."

And then Lena Singleton starts jogging away from me and says, "We'd better get going then!"

LENA

OK, so maybe I subconsciously headed to the same place I saw Alice running last time. I thought we might pass each other. I thought I might get a chance to say 'Hey'. I did not expect to find her having a little meltdown because her phone died. I was pretty surprised when she said she had been using a coaching app. That she'd only been running for seven weeks. I thought it was kind of amazing she'd just taken it upon herself to do it, but I got the feeling she didn't really want to talk about it. When she said she only had ten minutes more to complete her run I knew I couldn't let her quit.

"We'd better get going then!" I set off slowly, I wasn't sure what sort of pace she wanted to keep. She seemed a little unsure at the beginning. Running small quick steps then slowing down again. It was hard to run alongside her. She started muttering something under her breath like a mantra and soon her strikes were even and regular. I didn't try to chat to her. I could tell she was concentrating. When we got to five minutes, I said, "halfway there" and she gave me a little smile. I let her know when we were at two minutes, one minute and counted down the final ten seconds. She was breathing hard and trying to smile. She was laughing and coughing and holding her sides.

"Great job!" I said. "Smashed it."

She beamed and high fived me.

"Didn't we, though!?" she said. "Let's get snacks!"

We walked to Tesco Express. Alice bought a big bottle of chocolate milk and a chicken avocado sandwich.

She is my kind of people. I got Maltesers and Doritos. She went "yaaaas" when she saw my purchases. We sat on a wall outside and shared the lot.

"So, you go running all the time, right?" she said, a little accusingly. "I'm sorry if I ruined your run."

"Ha, no way! No worries. Actually, I've only recently taken up long distance running."

"Really?"

"Yep, even less than seven weeks ago."

"Well, I could tell you were struggling a little . . ."

I was floored for a second. Before she threw her head back and cackled into the cold night air. I could see her laughter. And then I could see mine.

"No, but honestly, Lena, thanks – you totally rescued my run. I wouldn't have completed tonight's session and I know it would have thrown my whole week."

"Really, it was no big thing."

We finished our snacks as we walked, and talked a bit about school. Alice didn't seem to know much about Aimee at all. Lucky Alice. She talked about her friends a little, but she talked more about some hilarious guy in her art class called Jacob Porter. Maybe she likes him. She laughed along to her own stories and it was infectious. Her laugh is so loud. I noticed how relaxed

I felt, and how much it did not feel like this to be with Aimee any more.

"Take a sweaty selfie with me. I'll give you my number."

She picks my phone from my hand and sends herself the photo. I'm not sure why she wants this blurry photo of our shiny faces but I like that she's added herself to my contacts.

"See you tomorrow!" she calls out as I turn off to my house. Like it was totally normal. Like we were friends.

A little while later my phone pings.

Alice: Hi Lena, if you could not mention to anyone that you saw me running that'd be great . . . I'm still a bit too rubbish for this to be in the public domain. Thanxxxxx *dies of exhaustion*

Lena: NOTHING rubbish about smashing a 25 minute run! You should be proud.

Alice: Well, of course I'm proud, but that's just between us. *Freddie Mercury moustache* WEEE ARE THE CHAAMPIONNNS, MY FRIIIEEENND.

MINNIE

I am watching another film starring the French actress. Mum was delighted at my suggestion. I've even left my phone in my bedroom so I'm not tempted to message Daniel and miss what everyone is saying. The actress is playing a woman scorned. She's been cheated on by her husband who is much older than her and not really very handsome at all, but he's managed to cheat on her with a much younger woman and our woman is really very angry about it. Mum and Dad keep making silly jokes about "not trying any of that round here". Mum can speak French so she sometimes replies to Dad in French and although I don't know exactly what she's saying I get the gist and it's super lovey-dovey. Dad only has a few basic words so he just agrees a lot and laughs in a cartoon French accent.

"How come you speak French so well, Mum?"

And then she drops this bombshell.

"I used to live in Paris."

Quoi?!

It turns out that Mum did a two-year placement at a French university! How did I not know that?

"How did I not know that?!"

She just says, "Of course you knew that," and I'm

wondering if maybe I did. Maybe I knew and I ignored it. Maybe it didn't seem relevant to me so I just didn't hear it. It hasn't got anything to do with netball.

"Tell me all about it!" I'm suddenly thrilled by the idea of Mum walking around Paris looking chic in plain white t-shirts. "Have you got photos?"

"Yes, I have. I will do, but can we finish the film first?"

"Oh yeah, *mais oui*!"

"*Bien!*"

The film is brilliant. The woman sets up a cunning trap for her husband and exposes his affair to all his friends and clients at a big business event. The young woman he's cheating with is the daughter of one of his biggest investors and he loses everything. My favourite part was how when she was royally stitching him up, she was wearing a man's tuxedo. She looked so super cool in it I had to Google image search for hours afterwards to try and find a still from the film of her wearing the suit. I saved it to my phone so I can keep looking at it. I feel like it's inspirational somehow. Not that I ever want to be a woman scorned, or hell-bent on revenge. But she looks so strong and powerful and honestly, like she doesn't give a flying f—

Daniel: Film finished? Want to go for a run?

Daniel and I have been doing a bit of light jogging to get me back into exercise. Just twenty minutes or so at a time. We've been a few times now and I really love it. My shoulder doesn't hurt any more and it feels good to be using my body again. Daniel talks and talks. I love hearing about what he did that day in class or things he read on the internet that he thinks are interesting. He loves learning about weird new materials being engineered in Japan that make prosthetic limbs and the giant printers that make them. He's interested in so many things.

We meet up at the park and he gives me a huge hug. His hugs are like his smiles. Warm and massive and a bit silly. He presses every inch of his body against me and squeezes until I start laughing.

"Hey, girl."

"Hey, boy, let's go!"

We jog gently around the park perimeter. Daniel tells me about how he's trying to fix his brother's moped as a surprise for his birthday.

"It still runs, but it makes this awful noise. I think it all just needs a really good clean. The best bit is, I know Mum has got him a new one because he told her it was bust and it's his twenty-first birthday, so the way I see it is, if I do a good fix-up job on the old one, he might just give it back to me for my birthday!" He's beaming. Who wouldn't give him a moped? We pass some other joggers who smile at us and some people from our school snogging on a bench. We smile at each other then. Daniel has football training in half an hour so after a few laps of the park he has to go. We have another little cuddle and he runs off into the distance, waving and spinning around to smile some more.

I decide to lap the park once more. The air is just the right temperature and everything feels calm and still. I punish myself for a few moments thinking about how I avoided collecting one of the applications for the French exchange *again* today. The deadline is looming and I can't seem to make myself even go and pick up the form. Somehow, I've convinced myself that applying would be an insult to Daniel – a long summer to spend with each other and I'm immediately leaving the country? How would I feel if he was doing that? I think I'd feel hurt. I think I'd be worried I wasn't enough. I couldn't do that to him. But . . . having the paperwork wouldn't commit me to anything. I wouldn't even have to tell anyone anything about it. I keep on running. I imagine the park is in Paris. I dodge cyclists carrying fresh bread in their baskets. I imagine little old men in felt berets calling *"Allo!"*

from park benches and their little dogs running alongside me. I imagine collapsing into a cafe after a long run in the spring sunshine and ordering *deux croissants.* Leafing through a French magazine. Dunking my croissant into a proper hot chocolate. Eating a salad in an art gallery canteen. Walking along the river with a shopping bag of vegetables. Browsing a bookshop wearing a wool coat. Calling out *"excusez-moi"* to the runners I pass. *Excusez-moi! Excusez-moi!*

I'm gaining on a small group of runners who have come out of nowhere. They're all wearing illuminated arm bands although it isn't dark yet, and there's one really lean guy at the front who seems to be leading the pack. He's wearing a bib over his running gear that says FIT4LIFE PT AND RUNNING COACH. The guy from the poster at school! This must be the running club they were advertising. Most of the runners are wearing headphones but a couple are chatting a little as they go. The coach signals to them that they're leaving the park at the next exit and they peel off on to the road with their armbands flashing in unison. In a total surprise to myself, I follow them. I have no idea why I'm doing this. I want to know where they're going, I suppose. Although I know the answer is simply, 'for a run'.

I'm keeping pace a few steps behind them and suddenly the leader drops through the group and runs alongside me.

"Hiya! I'm Leo. Are you joining us?"

And because I have no idea why else I'd be following them like this, I say, "yes, please, if that's OK?"

"We're glad to have you. You look like you know what you're doing but any worries let me know."

"Thanks. OK. Thanks." *Merci beaucoup.*

Every now and again he calls out an early direction to those of us without earphones in. Sometimes he congratulates us on doing well or comments that it's a beautiful evening. When the sun starts to get really low and everything looks twinkly and twilighty he shouts into the air, "I AM RUNNING!" and the whole group answers back with, "WE ARE RUNNING!" Which strikes me as both odd and totally reasonable at the same time. We are running. Like a pack of wolves. Strong, in sync, in control. It feels great.

After our road route, we loop back into the park for some cool-down stretches. I suddenly feel embarrassed and wish I had snuck off home when we were running.

Leo claps his hands and says, "Well done, everyone" and the rest of the group clap too. Everyone is smiling.

"We have a new runner too – everyone, this is Minnie!"

"Hi, Minnie!"

"Great job!"

"Nice to meet you!" Nice things echo around the neon-clad group, but I'm too dazed to respond. How does Leo know my name?

He comes over and hands me a flashing armband. "We meet here every evening at 5.30 p.m. Next time, wear this."

And in another move of total insanity, I take the armband from him, turn, and run.

ALICE

"Hi Jacob." I've accosted Jacob Altman by the bins. I had told myself I was going to say hi as soon as I saw him and then there he was, straight away, first thing in the morning, by the bins. No time to have even accumulated any litter. Too early for a Twix. Even for me – I'm not an animal. I scrounged around in my pocket for something to throw away and found a brand new unsneezed-on tissue and threw it in the bin saying a silent apology for the little bit of tree I had just wasted.

"Hi . . ." he said, crumpling something up suspiciously and forcing it into his pocket so frantically it misses entirely and lands on the ground between us. ". . . Alice."

I look down. It's one of the new school bookmarks using the photos from THAT DAY. God, that means all the photos will be out there now. This one stars my two tiny sporty faux friends, running down the racetrack. Nice choice, Jacob. Clearly Snow White likes his girls like he likes his woodland animals. Small and cute and fast...

"Well, see you in Art, then," I say, because I'm annoyed with him now.

"OK..."

I wait.

"...Alice."

Phenomenal.

I find Jodie and Caro by some other bins on the other side of the school. Thankfully we've been friends for years and I don't need to make any more fake rubbish. "Wha g'wan," I say as I slump down, and they both talk a million miles an hour about how they might sort of have dates for the ball.

"Wha?? G'wan!!" I say. And they look a bit dumb so I change to a *Grease* theme, "Tell me more, tell me more..."

Apparently, Marcus and Kevin from their lolz

Social Studies class are a bit cute and Marcus told Jodie that Kevin likes Caro and Caro told Kevin that Jodie likes Marcus then Marcus told Kevin that he likes Jodie and Jodie told Caro that she likes Kevin and now they're all going to go to the ball together because it'd be so much fun to 'just go as friends'.

I'm still trying to unscramble that ludicrous love quadrangle when Jacob Porter runs over screaming, "ALIIIICE" and throws his arms around my neck, which is exactly the response I had hoped for from Other Jacob, but with less sass. Actually, that response would have been nice from Jodie or Caro, now I'm thinking of it.

"Have you seen the photos?? We look FLAWLESS. You can barely even tell I'm wearing make-up!" Those photos are the last things I want to go and look at now. He turns and acknowledges Jodie and Caro.

"Hello, girls!" before turning back to me and stage-whispering, "So, are you ditching us to be best friends with Lena Singleton now?" Jodie and Caro stop squealing and turn to us, waiting for my answer.

"Um, no?" But now I have to have a reason why I was with her last night and it can't be that she was my stand-in running coach because Jodie and Caro are still here and for whatever reason I still don't want them to know about that. Also, how does that pesky pixie even know I was with her last night?!

"We've been friends for ages," I start the lie with absolutely no idea where it'll take me, "we're in the same tech group."

Which is true, but that group then got split into five separate mini-groups on the first day of term and we have never been in the same one since.

"It's just you looked SO cosy in your photos with her and Minnie Michaels." Oh, yeah, right, *those* photos. "Panic over, girls." Jacob says to Caro and Jodie, who don't really look worried at all.

Lena Singleton takes this opportunity to walk through our eyeline with totally inappropriate timing so I'm forced to shout and wave, "Hi Lena, see you in tech!" to prove my lie and she gives me this wild-eyed look like 'shut up!' I try to send her a telepathic explanation along the lines of 'only the running bit was the bit I wanted to hide, please don't pretend that you don't know me, we're going with "we are old tech friends", k thanks,' and then realise that's too long for a telepathic message so I send her a text during registration.

Why couldn't she just meet me by some bins so I could explain it to her properly . . .

LENA

Aimee is still grumpy with me for walking away from her the other day, but when Alice Daly-Donne shouts over to me across the playground at school, Aimee flips her lid. "What is it with you and Big Alice?"

"Nothing," I say. Is it something?

"Oh my god!" We're cutting through main reception when we see it. When Aimee sees it. She assesses the situation. I actually see her calculating the options; how can she handle this best so I'm kept in my place. "You must be SO embarrassed."

The photos are much bigger than I expected. I didn't know they were going to be used on other things – I thought it was just for some brochure. Our faces are on huge all-weather vinyl banners. They're on tall signs that have their own metal stands. They're on bunting and bookmarks and plastic document holders, for crying out loud. Mounted on a giant blue pinboard are the original photographs. The whole lot of them. Every fake smile, fake conversation, fake high five, fake race; me in my fake life.

"Ha ha ha, you and Skinny Minnie look so tiny next to Big Alice."

"Don't call her that!" I snap.

"What, do you fancy her or something, now? You used to call her that too, you know."

"I know! I wish I hadn't. It's just mean, Aimee. Why do we have to be mean?"

Aimee looks totally startled. I've never said anything like this to her. And because I don't know what I've unleashed, I just do it again. I bolt.

When I get to my class, I have a message from Alice on my phone and I tap out a quick reply.

Do you want to go for a run sometime?

I'm sitting next to Seb and he's being funny and charming. I can see why Aimee likes him so much. I feel light and buzzy. Like I'm changing. I'm making the move, I've decided. I'm going to break out of Aimee's web. Maybe Tasha and Nikki will come with me, but if they don't want to, that's fine too. I'm going to be friends with Alice. I'm going to go running with Alice. I might even be friends with Seb. If that's possible.

Alice: Can't go tonight but I have my RunTime session scheduled for tomorrow if you want to join me?

Sounds good.

I need to go running tonight anyway. I'll go to Dad's club.

MINNIE

I stared at the photos for a long time, wondering why they felt off, somehow. Was I actually that happy back then? Because I looked *really* happy. Too happy. A smiling girl with pristine kit, aiming for the stars or whatever the naff slogan said I was doing. Laughing with my teammates; shooting those goals, celebrating those wins. Running races; believing and achieving. Hanging with my friends; a picture of positivity; *Striving for Success!*

But the smiles in the fake friends photographs are no different to the smiles in my team photographs. Apparently, that's my go-to expression, applicable in all situations. I can't tell those girls apart and that depresses me. How can that be the real me? I guess that's just the face I put on to please other people. It looks just like me, but I'm not there at all ...

Captain Bella interrupted my crisis. When was I coming back to practice? When was I going to be ready to play for the club again? Why wasn't I coming to do drills with the team? Didn't the doctor give me the all clear to play again? Didn't I miss everyone? Wasn't I pumped for next season?

All I could give her was 'not sures' and 'don't knows'. She got frustrated with me.

"Come on, Minnie. What's the problem?!" And I couldn't explain it to her because what could I say that wasn't going to sound ridiculous? I can't come to netball because I've realised I don't know who I am any more? Worst excuse ever. I fibbed some fluff about having a physio appointment but I think I told someone else it was a family birthday so if they add it all up, they'll know it was just lies. I come home from school feeling thoroughly miserable.

As if she knew I needed it, Mum is waiting in the kitchen with a photo album and a cafetière of hot coffee. She's also baked these little shell sponge cakes called madeleines, which she says we should dip into the coffee. They are sweet and delicious and make the coffee taste dark and sophisticated. We look through the photo album together and she points out the sights and tells me little anecdotes about the places she went and the people she met. I was disappointed to see she did not look particularly chic while she was there, having a penchant for hippy crochet cardigans over polo neck jumpers and a lot of brown corduroy.

"You are actually named after a friend I had in Paris."

"You're kidding! Tell me!"

"Well, don't be upset, but Minnie was the name of my landlady's cat. Trust me, she was a very beautiful cat and Madame Brodeteaux adored her. Minnie *le chat* would always come into my room and sleep on my bed when I wasn't home. I would leave the window open for her and she would keep my pillow warm. I would give her the cream out of my eclairs, because if it's a well-filled eclair it will squidge out when you bite it. She had beautiful blue eyes, like you. She was just warm and small and lovely, which is exactly how I described you when you were born and the name just fitted. I never told your dad where it came from!"

When it gets to 5.15 p.m. something goes off in me like an alarm. I hadn't planned to go to the club. I spent all day convincing myself I definitely wasn't going to go and then as soon as I was in danger of being late, I was lacing on my trainers in a frenzy. I ran to the park before I could reason with myself and Leo saw me and gave me a big smiley wave.

"Minnie, you made it, great to see you." Oh god, I had forgotten he knew who I was.

"See, Lena, I told you she'd be here. Now you can run together."

LENA

The thing was, he hadn't told me she would be there. I wouldn't have been there if he had. He knew that. I was furious with him. He smiled and squeezed my shoulder as he addressed the group.

"We're on a nice long route tonight. Low and slow as you like. Let's enjoy it. Off we go!"

As if.

I thunder away. I position myself next to Dad's fittest and fastest client. Imagining I can keep up with him for the whole route is a fantasy but I need to show Minnie I am boss here. This is *my* home turf. *My* running club.

I keep my eyes focused ahead. I pound the tarmac with my frustration. What is she doing here? *I* run long distance. She's a sprinter. She shouldn't even be here. What is she thinking? Can't I just have this one thing without her overshadowing me? And in front of my dad too? I hear myself in Aimee's voice. 'Eugh, what is she thinking?' I push forward again and I feel my chest starting to tighten. I can't maintain this pace for another minute, let alone another mile.

I stop and look around. I'm out on my own. I've bolted from the group leaving Dad and the rest of the club in my dust. I bend over and heave the evening into my lungs.

It hurts. I've run off the planned route and I turn to see the group snaking out of the park and on to the road.

I think about how immature I look. How I've embarrassed my Dad in front of all of his clients. How Minnie will think I'm scared to run with her. I think about how cruel Aimee is. And how Alice isn't. Alice who runs. Because running is for everyone. I feel angry and miserable and hopeless in an instant and because I don't know what else to do, I shout out in to the air. "AARRRGHHHHH!"

And because he's amazing, Dad answers my cry.

"I. AM. RUNNING!!!"

And then the club do too.

"WE. ARE. RUNNING!!!"

They are just outside the park walls. They've followed the perimeter round and they're just coming level with me now. If I'm fast and I take the next exit I can join them before they cross at the lights. I'm cringing but I'm running again. Sprinting as if my life depends on it. Maybe it does. Maybe the life where I'm bitter and jealous like Aimee can stay in the park and I can escape it if I make it back to the group before the lights. I dig deep and then I dig some more. I feel like a wild animal, frightened and desperate. I charge through the next set of gates and scan around. I can't see them. I can't see them. The traffic lights change and they've already gone. It feels like I've missed my chance to become a good person.

"Lena!!!"

I turn around and there they are. Softly streaming towards me in the twilight. Smiling faces. Warm and open. Dad, beaming.

"Wrong way, babe. Glad you found us. Remember, low and slow."

"You're a good coach, Dad."

He pats me on the head as he slides past me. The group flows around me like a brook. I'm a stone. Stuck in a moment. At the back of the group is Minnie.

I take a breath and start running next to her. Low and slow.

"Hey, Minnie."

Low and slow.

ALICE

The ball is just a week away and Other Jacob has not invited me despite 'liking' all of my casual posts about how I'm definitely going. He has probably asked some tiny bunny girl with big eyelashes. It wasn't until Caro and Jodie mentioned going with Whatshisname and Whatshisface that I even thought about needing a date. Now they have dates and I don't, so I guess I'm not going with them any more. Even though we had those plans where we wore old people's clothes. Did I remember that wrong?

"Do you have a date for the ball?" I ask my favourite pixie.

"Of course, I haven't. No one has. Apart from that girl Minnie and her boyfriend who are an actual couple, and that's not called a date because they've been going out for ages." Jacob Porter knows about these things.

"Right? Right!"

"Why? Who thinks they've got a date?"

"Well, Caro and Jodie said they have got dates!"

"With who? Swedish Ant and Dec?" (Kevin and Marcus are quite blonde and Nordic looking, and short.) "Absolute rubbish. This is just one of those things where the girls think it's a date and the boys have no clue which one they're even meant to like. They've just agreed that they are going, and they already were because everyone in the whole year is. That's not a date."

"I think you're right. Poor Caro and Jodie. Should I tell them?"

"No, darling. Let them have their fantasy. It's kinder that way."

"So, they still think they have dates and that I'm a loser."

"Yes, darling . . ." he gives me a wicked look and bursts into laughter.

My phone pings and I look down to see he has messaged me. How did I fail to notice he was typing while we were having that conversation?

Jacob Porter: Will you be my date to the ball?

"Ha!! You goof. I'm going to say yes and now you have to pick me up and bring me a small flower on a hair bobble to wear round my wrist and you can't dance with anyone else all night or I will throw a FIT."

Jacob agrees to my terms and we spend the rest of the lesson cackling like witches because we are the only people in the whole year who actually have dates. We post a photo to celebrate.

Other Jacob likes it and it feels like the final nail in the coffin of our relationship. What a disappointment that was. I'm glad I didn't tell Juliet about him. She's always asking if I like anyone.

"Yes," I always tell her. "I like you, I like Mum and Dad, I like Phillip, I guess Clara's OK, I like Drake,

I like Claudia Winkleman . . ." Until she tells me to shut up and/or throws something at me.

I'm meeting Juliet after school. She's taking me to the shopping centre to find something to wear. As well as ditching me for their 'dates' ho ho ho, they've also ditched our plans to get vintage dresses. They sent me photos in a group chat of them trying on identical stretchy Lycra dresses and sky-high heels pulling really sad faces saying: We know these aren't really you but they are **REALLY** us. Plz 4give us xxxxxx ps. Do we look hot though?

They did, I guess. In the way they wanted to.

Like Ariana Grande, I replied. Which I know they will love. I am not ready to look so sexualised. I guess it has something to do with having a body that people feel entitled to comment on from passing cars. I'm always trying to find ways to look younger, or look my age at least. Their bodycon dresses show off their tiny frames and flat chests and I immediately have images of dirty old men looking at their photos on the internet. Men with The Face.

Juliet is waiting for me with a chai latte in a take-out cup. I give her one of the new bookmarks with my photo on and she hoots with laughter. "It is so mad how you can be SO gorgeous and SUCH A GEEK at the same time." I try and snatch it back off her she but crams it into her pocket.

She smooths my hair down and smiles, "You're going to break so many hearts with this beautiful face . . . I hate you! But I love you! . . . but I hate you!"

"But you love me. Now, shut up and let's go shopping."

She says we're doing one lap of window shopping only, then we can go back to three shops that we like the vibe of. She says I should try lots of styles on and I've got to try on anything that she picks out. We toast our deal with the lattes and slurp it through the little hole that probably isn't really for drinking from.

The deal goes out the window when Juliet stops at the first shop window and shouts, "HOLD THE PHONE, I'VE FOUND IT". I hold her chai latte instead as she charges into the shop and starts undressing the mannequin in the window. She motions at the drinks through the window. "Get rid of those and come and try this on."

I decide that putting the two nearly full cups down *behind* a bin is better than putting them in it and not just littering because if someone were to find them that would be a nice surprise. Juliet thrusts an item of clothing at me and I'm in the changing room unfolding it before I even work out what it is.

"A jumpsuit!?"

"Put it on!"

"For jumping?!"

"Put it on!"

"Or is a romper for a really giant baby?"

"Put it on!"

I put it on and turn around to the mirror and suddenly . . . music is playing and I shake my hair loose which is perfectly blow-dried and I've got a face full of sultry make-up and obviously I'm an absolute vision . . .

OK, so without the magical hairdo and make-up, I actually do look really good in this weird baby jumping suit. It's a kind of shimmery green colour, which sounds reptilian but even I can tell it looks good on my skin. It has wide loose cropped legs which skim over my 'athletic' thighs, even though they really are athletic now. I'm not really afraid of them any more. It has a pretty neckline with a bit of fuss and it's not too low. It definitely looks like a party outfit but it feels as comfortable as house clothes. Juliet is a genius.

"I am a genius!" she shouts when I tiptoe out of the cubicle.

"It's true."

"Chai lattes to celebrate!"

With any luck, they're still out there . . . and maybe even still a little warm.

MINNIE

So, it turns out Leo is Lena Singleton's dad! He knew me from school athletics club so I guess Lena must have mentioned me at home at some point. I think I must have been wrong about the thing at BurgerShack. It doesn't seem like Lena hates me at all. We did the whole route together and ended up chatting quite a lot. I think she had a timed sprint thing to complete first, but when she rejoined the group she started running alongside me. I asked her about the club and it turns out she is actually quite new to long distances too. I think we had both been feeling a bit bored by the competitive sprinting at school.

"I just want to run for me, you know?" she said. I knew exactly what she meant. Running in the pack and the lovely warm evening made me feel good in a way that I haven't been able to recently and I found myself talking and talking. About netball. About Daniel. I even mentioned the France thing. I actually heard myself say that I want to see Paris and I'm starting to feel like maybe I should go there to sort of, find myself, or something. I realised after a while she had barely said a word and I was cringing.

"Oh god, I need to shut up. Did you want to run ahead or run in silence?"

"No, no, it's cool. I'm listening."

She *was* listening. "Thanks."

I got tired towards the end of the run, it was much further than I had run before and more exercise than I'd done in months. I had to slow my pace.

"Are you all right?"

"Yeah, it's fine. I'm just getting tired. It's a shock to the system after moping around the house for weeks on end."

"We can slow down."

We fell into a really light jog and watched the rest of the group turn back in to the park ahead of us. They were doing their stretches when we caught up with them and Leo smiled at us both and said, "Great job, girls," giving Lena this lovely proud dad look. I get a good feeling about him.

"Thanks again, Mr Singleton, I really enjoyed it tonight." I say as I'm getting ready to leave. "And I'll see you at school tomorrow, Lena?"

"Sure thing."

I walk back home feeling a little heavy limbed but a little lighter in my heart. Lena hadn't laughed when I said I loved the idea of going to France after college just like my mum did – she asked if I was going to apply for the French Exchange Summer Programme and gave me this funny look when I said I wasn't sure.

"Oh? But the deadline is soon though, yeah?" she said. Yeah, it is. But she didn't roll her eyes when I said Daniel was the best thing that ever happened to me, and she laughed when I said I knew it was a bit cringe to say that. She seems to really understand about the netball thing. The pressure. I wonder if she gets any from her dad about her running, but he seems so friendly and relaxed it is hard to imagine. Wherever she is feeling it from, she said that in the short time she'd been doing it, that running outside of school had really helped her.

"It's like, quiet time . . . for me," she said, and I apologised again for spoiling it with my talking.

"No, it's quiet time for the body or something. Everything just loosens up. It's like getting a massage. I just feel better afterwards. Peaceful."

I thought about that as I walked back. Quiet time for my body. It was a funny way to think about something so active but that is always how being active has made me feel. Alive and happy and, somehow, peaceful. But that's running and cycling, swimming or climbing.

That's weekend stuff. It isn't netball. Playing the game is such a small part of that world, and the world is overpowering. Suffocating. The opposite of getting a massage. A twisted knot.

I think about the list I made for myself and realise, to my delight, I've ticked one item off! I've joined a club. I already know it is the right fit for me. I want to keep going. And the next thing on the list is to make a new friend. Perhaps I can get a half tick on that one for now.

LENA

OK, so I've been a total idiot. About everyone and everything. Minnie is genuinely a nice person and has been all along. And not arrogant about her talents at all. I've been the arrogant one. Assuming she was out to get me. She is only out to get herself. (Like me.) We should both take a lesson from Alice.

I didn't tell Minnie about Alice because running is still her secret. I'm hoping that Alice will join the running club when she feels ready. I think she already is, but she's set her own target and I respect that.

I'm buzzing all day at school. I've got my session with Alice tonight and then I'll see Minnie again tomorrow at running club. We already agreed we'd run together again.

She messaged me her number so we can arrange which nights we're going. I assumed we wouldn't talk at school so it caught me off guard when she came to find me at lunchtime.

"Are you going to the cafeteria, Lena?" Right there, in front of everyone.

"Yeah."

"Cool. Can I join you? I'm starving."

And she actually is. She gets a sandwich, crisps, fruit, yoghurt and a Yorkie. It is clear to me we are going to become true friends.

I ask Tasha and Nikki to come with us. I give them a look that I want to mean 'come on, be brave, leave her'. But they choose not to. I walk away with Minnie and I hear them snickering over their rice cakes.

"Thanks," I say, without realising I said it out loud.

"What for?" she says.

I just laugh, and she does too. Alice walks by with Jacob Porter and I smile and give a little wave. Alice does this weird thing where she stops in her tracks, looks all around her and then gives me this over-the-top fake wink and goes 'shhhh!' with her finger to her lips. Then she laughs and waves like a children's TV presenter, shouting, "SEE YOU LATER, LENA!"

I have a class with Seb after lunch. He has this lovely straightforward way of talking.

"So, Lena, obviously, I would like to ask you to be my date to the ball next week."

I did not see that coming. I like Seb. More than I like any other boy, for sure. But it doesn't feel like *that*. I enjoy his company. I want us to be friends. Proper friends. But I don't think there is any more to it.

"But, obviously, you aren't going to do that. Because we're good friends."

"Exactly right." He says with a smile. He looks a bit shy for the first time ever.

He moves on to a new topic of conversation and I look at his ears. His chin. His grey eyes. He has a nice face. If I was going to be interested in any boy, it would probably be him. Maybe I will be, one day? It is nice to know he likes me. But as I let the warmth of that sink in, I realise that he was never interested in Aimee. Despite everything, that makes me feel a little sad for her.

As I pass the school office after final period, I find myself collecting an application form for the Paris Exchange Summer Programme. I'm going to post it through

Minnie's door on the way home. I'm going to help her do this. Because she deserves it, and because she might not make it happen for herself. Because it's nice to have someone who is on your side. Because Aimee would never do it for me. Because Alice totally would.

Why do I feel like we'll all be wearing t-shirts that say BE MORE ALICE on them one day . . .?

MINNIE

As I open the front door, I catch some post under the door. The door drags the paper into scrunches as I try and release it – I really hope it's nothing important. It's a royal mess by the time I'm inside and holding it in my hand, and then I'm not sure I want to unscrunch it because I think I know exactly what it is . . .

A chance to step out on my own? A few weeks to breathe and take in new things? Sights, sounds, new people and new pastries? Or maybe loneliness. And awkwardness. Embarrassment. A whole giant space where Daniel Turner should be. Even worse, beautiful French boys who try to make me forget about Daniel Turner. What if I'm *that* girl? But, the Eiffel Tower. The Seine. The cafes on the streets. The women in their clothes. The vanilla ice cream and the cup of espresso . . .

I smooth out the application forms and decide to read them through properly. But first, coffee!

ALICE

I've got another twenty-five-minute run to complete tonight and my coach is going to be my old-buddy-from-Tech, Lena Singleton. Sorry, Sarah, you're temporarily dumped.

Lena's lucky that I can't chat as easily as she can when we're running so she gets a chance to tell me her life story. But those are never that long when you're a teenager. I prod her for more details on some things but she's not one for much elaboration. I nearly trip over myself when she casually says someone asked her out today.

"Why were you telling me about all that other stuff when there was potential romance in the air?!" I say. I also take this opportunity to add that Jacob Altman has not asked me out.

"I think Sebastian Edwards asked me to go to the ball with him, but I sort of made him take it back. So it wouldn't be weird."

"To be honest, Lena, forcing someone to rewind the

conversation is the weird bit. Playing Jedi mind tricks on helpless young boys who want to throw themselves at your feet. That was the weird bit. You are the weird bit. Why did you do that? Don't you like him? Also, I am going to tell Jacob Porter that people do ask people on dates to the ball. You are proof. So, don't you like him?"

"Yeah, I like him. But only like I like other people."

"Ah, like how I like Claudia Winkleman. Got it."

"Do you fancy Claudia Winkleman?! I thought you liked Jacob Altman!"

"I do like Jacob, but if I liked girls, maybe I'd go for Claudia!"

"That's probably how I feel about Seb."

"Claudia has better hair than him."

"I'm not deciding between them."

"OK. How much longer?"

We have another gruelling fifteen minutes to run so I whinge about Other Jacob a little bit and try to tell Lena the ballad of Caro and Jodie and Swedish Ant and Dec but in the end, I have to choose actual breathing over finishing the story.

We're running in deep, concentrated silence for the final four minutes when, unbelievably and might I add, ridiculously, that sneak with the camera appears again! I mean, this counts as stalking now, right? I actually see a person this time, although it's just a dark dark figure in a dark dark jacket with a dark dark hood pulled around their face . . . which is obscured by a camera. But he doesn't take a photo this time. He turns suddenly and scurries away. Presumably with his rat-tail dragging after him. I feel sort of offended, and then confused, maybe he was never taking a photo of me? Then, none of that matters because I am in agony, my sippy cup is empty and we still have three minutes to go.

When we complete the run with little fanfare (seriously, Lena, where's my fanfare?) she tries to pick up the conversation again.

"So, you're annoyed with them?"

And I forget all about the rat because I realise I'm genuinely not annoyed with Caro and Jodie at all.

"Nah. I've got this slinky lizardy outfit and I'm going to go with Jacob Porter, which will be hilarious, and I'm really looking forward to it. You'll be there too, *not with Sebastian Edwards*, so you can crash our date if you like. Jacob's gay anyway."

Lena looks pretty chuffed that I've asked her to join

us and it dawns on me that she wants us to be mates IRL. How nice is that? It's a funny thing at our age, to get new mates. You feel like you've got to stick with the ones you've got because that's the way it was when you were little, but actually things change a lot during high school. You become different people and want to look different and it makes perfect sense that you'd want new friends as part of that package. Running Alice has a running friend, of course she does. And it's an actual person, Lena Singleton, not podcast Sarah. Who I do feel a bit bad about ditching to be honest. How will she know that I've completed this twenty-five-minute run without her counting me through it? Maybe I'll play the podcast later when I dry my hair, just so it hasn't got an unlistened-to-track. Stuff like that bugs me.

It's only when I'm at home later – in my pyjamas, eating jammy toast and listening to Sarah tell me that I'm doing brilliantly – that I realise how much my running has improved. I have just two more weeks to complete the app and then I will legit be a runner who goes running and is actually decent. Result!

MINNIE

I've agreed to go to netball practice tonight, even though

every part of me feels like it's a bad idea. I was sitting in my room, about to read the application for France, when Captain Bella phoned me, actually called me to speak to, and put me on the spot right there and then.

"Are you coming to practice tonight?" and I had to say OK.

Sophie gives me a little hug when I get there, "Yay, you're here!" and Captain Bella gives this rousing team talk before we start, saying that now I'm back, we are on to be regional champions next season. She reminds us that the county coaches will see us play again and stares at me hard, like, 'I'm talking to you, Michaels!'

We do some drills and then play a game, and honestly, it isn't as bad as I thought it would be. I don't feel stressed about it and my shoulder feels absolutely fine. But when it comes to the end and we talk about the upcoming season and all the fixtures, I realise I have no intention of playing them. I have made up my mind and that is all there is to it. In my head, and my body, netball is just something I used to do.

"It's just how I feel."

"But I don't understand what has changed! Your shoulder is better now. You played great tonight. As always!" Captain Bella is resisting my resignation.

"I've just decided I don't want to play any more. There's nothing you can do to change my mind. I'm sorry, Bella."

Bella is at a loss, but she's a reasonable person and she can see that no amount of shouting at me or repeating herself is going to change my mind at this particular moment.

"I'm going to check with you about this again later," she says sternly.

"OK," I agree. Wondering if there is any chance in this world that I could change my mind again. Might I wake up feeling totally different again? I feel resolute now, but if you'd asked me three months ago if I was sure I wanted to play county netball, I'd have said yes. Teenagers cannot be trusted with grand statements. We should just stop making them.

Daniel is waiting for me with a KitKat. "Good practice?" he says. I kiss him instead of answering.

"You're not going back, are you?"

I stop and look at him, a finger of KitKat halfway to my lips. "How did you know that?"

"Because you didn't bounce out. You weren't excited to go. You've come out early which means you aren't staying to chat to the girls. You don't message them in the evenings anymore. You're done."

"Do you think I'm doing the wrong thing?"

"Nah, babe. Staying if you didn't want to would be wrong." He wraps his arm around my shoulder and we set off home. Why would I ever want to be in a different country to Daniel Turner?

"Hey, boy?"

"Yeah, girl?"

"I love you."

LENA

Alice wants to finish week eight of her app before the ball on Friday, so we cram her sessions into the first half of the week and I miss running club. Minnie couldn't go anyway. I float the idea of Alice joining the club but she won't commit to anything. And definitely not before she completes the programme. She always uses this term 'runner' like it's something she's still yet to become. Even when she's physically running.

We're near the end of our second twenty-eight-minute run of the week but Alice is struggling. She's breathing hard and heavy. No chatting. This one has been a real slog for her. I try to tell her we all have bad runs. It doesn't mean anything. It's just this one, today. She shoots me angry eyes and huffs loudly. She stomps along the tarmac. Losing her form, slapping her feet down with furious determination.

"But you're still running!" I tell her. I try to think what my dad would say. She's slowing down.

"I. Hate. This!" she says, and I'm worried I'm going to lose her. We're so close. I check my watch and it's two minutes to go. I don't know if telling her this would finish her off or fire her up. How does Dad do this? I want to let her stop. I can't let her stop!

"You're doing so great, Alice. You are amazing. Look how far you've come in just eight weeks. Remember how hard it felt at the beginning?"

"It. Feels. Like. That. Now!"

Damn.

"We can't give up now, Alice. You'll only have to do it all over again if you do."

"RAT!!!!" She suddenly shouts. "RAT! RAT! RAT!"

"Is this like a chanting thing?" I ask. Should I join in?

"The rat! He's taking photographs of us!" She's pointing wildly into the darkness and I wonder if she's delirious, but then I see what she's pointing at. In the distance, in the dark, there's a person with a camera.

"RUN!" Alice roars, and out of nowhere she picks up the pace. She runs off the path and into the grass towards the figure. She's surging forward and I'm caught off guard so I sprint to catch up with her. She's possessed.

"What's going on?" I ask when I'm next to her again.

"He's papping us!" she huffs.

"But why?" I say.

"Don't know! Let's . . . Find . . . Out!" She manages before she suddenly slams to a halt and falls to her knees, blowing deep hot breaths. She's burnt herself out with that sudden sprint.

"Alice, are you OK?"

"Catch. Him!" she says, as she lies back in the damp grass.

I check my watch. Twenty-eight minutes and eight seconds.

"Alice, you did it."

She manages a smile. "Course. I. Did," she says. "Now. RUN!"

And I do. I take off like a firework. I zig-zag wildly through the grass and see the opening to the houses on the other side. He must have gone through there. I power forward and leap out in the space, expecting to see my target more clearly, and instead I crash straight into Minnie and Daniel Turner.

The houses behind the field are old and posh. They run in a big cul-de-sac and then lead off in a strip alongside an alley. Unless our creep lives in one of these mansions, he's got to be still here.

I grab Minnie's arm and explain the situation as we start running. Daniel runs alongside too.

"You go left and I'll go right, and whoever gets to him first can keep hold of him until the other catches up."

Minnie looks unsure. Daniel looks excited.

"Got it!" he shouts as he starts running, dragging Minnie behind him.

MINNIE

Daniel is loving this. We are running around the houses, checking down the sides and calling to each other.

"All clear!"

"Roger that!"

If there is a creep with a camera hiding round here, he definitely knows we're looking for him. And that we aren't much of a threat. I don't really know what we'd even do if we saw him. Chase him down and then what? Pin him down on the ground? Call the police? Is it illegal to take a photograph of someone you don't know? Hopefully Daniel's got a plan for that bit.

"Do you see anyone?" I call out, hoping he hasn't.

"Not a dickie bird."

Phew. "Maybe we should go back and find Alice. What if she has found the guy?"

"If Alice has found him, it's him that needs our help."

We run quickly around the loop of houses we're in, then head back to the centre of the cul-de-sac to collect Lena and go and find Alice. Chances are, whoever it was has taken the alley and is long gone.

Except he isn't. He's right there. Having a conversation with Lena. And we know him.

ALICE

I'm jogging on the spot when Lena comes back to find me. Looks like she's picked up a friend on the way. "I'm FREEZING! Did you catch him? Have you got any snacks? Hi, Minnie. The gang's all back together – say a kind of cheese! But really, I'm glad you're OK after your accident. I saw you in the ambulance actually – true story. Can I borrow your jacket?"

"Oh yeah, of course!" She gives me her oversized fleece (it fits snugly) and says she knows how it feels when the sweat turns cold on your skin. I wonder if I should apologise for putting cold sweat inside her fleece but she says, "Check the pockets," and I am thrilled to find some Smarties in there.

"One of us! One of us!" I chant in Lena's direction while

pointing the tube at Minnie, shaking it like a tambourine.

Minnie laughs, but in the way you would laugh at a clown you were secretly frightened of.

"So, did you find him?" I ask Lena. I don't know how much Minnie knows.

"No," Minnie answers before Lena can. "No sign of him anywhere."

Sneaky rat. Where did you go?

"Are you scared?" Minnie asks me, genuinely concerned.

"Only that whoever it is will post the pics online!" I say. "Running is our secret, isn't it, Lena? And now yours too, Minnie Michaels. Don't tell anyone. Also, why are you here?"

Lena explains how she crashed into Minnie when she was hot on the tail of the rat and how, heroically, Minnie joined the search but that the target was nowhere to be seen.

Fair enough.

"SO, we need to celebrate the fact you completed your run this evening!" Lena says.

Oh yeah! We totally do because it was an absolute brute and I am basically the personification of strength and determination for pushing through that.

Lena explains to Minnie that I had "one of those runs where you just hit the wall" and amazingly, Minnie looks she actually understands that feeling and it wasn't something that Lena made up just to make me feel better. I wonder if I should tell her that I say a little secular prayer to her every time I run, but decide that would sound terrifying.

"Oh god, yeah, we've all had those. It's so hard to keep going. Well done, you!" Minnie says, before adding this belter: "I live just over there. Celebration hot chocolate and toast at mine?"

LENA

We're walking back to Minnie's house, laughing and chatting like those three girls in the photos. Like friends in real life. Minnie gets a few texts and mouths that it's Daniel and she'll explain later. She gives a little thumbs up and a smile. Whatever it is, it's fine. And we have a little secret.

Alice is admiring Minnie's trainers and then, in a conversation jump invisible to us, she suddenly asks me, "What are you going to wear to the ball?"

I still haven't picked anything. I'd never gone shopping with Aimee because those planned days out never seemed to happen. I don't have a big sister to borrow something off, and I don't have time to order anything online. I feel angry at myself for not thinking about this properly. What did I think would happen? That I'd just throw on something from my wardrobe, which is all joggers and hoodies, and it'd be the perfect thing?

I don't think I can ask Nikki or Tasha, they're still Team Aimee.

I think about asking Alice if I can come and borrow something from her but let's face it, she's at least a foot taller than I am. Nothing she owns is going to fit me.

"I . . . I don't know?" I say. Gormless. Clueless.

And without missing a beat Minnie says, "You can have a look through my stuff if you want to borrow something. I've got loads of formal wear from all my cousins' weddings and going out with the netball team. We'll find you something."

I feel myself flush, hot and embarrassed. I feel myself about to blurt out something like, "No no, it's fine. I've got something, I'm sure". But instead I decide to just shut up and accept the help. Accept the fact that Minnie Michaels wants to help me. Accept that Minnie Michaels is my friend.

Alice loves rifling through Minnie's wardrobe. She laughs at all of Minnie's petite clothes and tries on a few things and then stumbles around the room pretending to be the hulk because Minnie's clothes make Alice look like she is bursting out of them. We drink hot chocolates and Minnie's mum brings us peanut butter on toast. She seems really happy that Minnie has friends round.

"I wish we were the same shoe size!" Alice groans. "I can't get my canal boats in any of your elf shoes and I'm basically going to have to wear my school shoes to the ball."

"Alice, you're going to look amazing, whatever you wear on your feet," Minnie says. And I can tell she really means it.

Alice and Minnie pull out a few dresses for me to try on. They're all nice, to be honest. I'd be happy in any of them. Anything like these feel really special when you live in sweats.

"I think I've got it!" Minnie says, producing a plain, teal dress in a stretchy fabric. It feels really smooth, almost like sports material. It's slim and fitted and the only design is a silver stripe running down the sides. I love it.

She finds some silver shoes to match. Of course, we're the same size. And even a little bag for my phone and lip gloss.

"You look incredible in that, Lena!" I'm too embarrassed to say thank you.

"Should I wear my hair up or down?" I ask.

"Down, definitely. Let those amazing curls out! I've always been so jealous of your hair."

Minnie Michaels has been jealous of me . . .

"Which one are you going to wear, Minnie?" Alice asks.

"It's a surprise!" she says. And she looks a little coy. Like she's got a really good secret.

"Fair enough," Alice says, trying on some of Minnie's stretchy gym clothes and admiring herself in the mirror.

"I'm looking forward to seeing it!" I say. And I really mean it.

We all change back into our own clothes and Minnie brings us these delicious milky coffees that taste of Nutella and little French cake things. She seems so sophisticated sometimes. We go back to her room and lounge around chatting about running and school and half watching some dumb reality show.

Minnie has one of the school bookmarks on her desk and Alice picks it up, flipping it over in our faces. "Look at this! You two running for your life on one side and me, Queen of the Nerds, on the other side!!!"

"The photographer didn't know that you were a double threat!" I say with a smile.

"Ha! But I wasn't . . . back then!"

"Oh, I hate all those stupid photos," Minnie says, pushing it off her desk and into the bin. "Do you want some noodles? I'm a bit peckish!" Girl can eat!

We end up staying for hours. She puts a movie on, "just for background noise while we chat", which I like. No pressure to talk, no pressure to watch. The movie is in French anyway so we can keep an eye on what is going on even if we do talk. I've never watched a subtitled movie before. Minnie clearly loves it. Alice reads the words aloud in an exaggerated French accent. Every now and again Minnie says something like, 'Doesn't France look amazing?' and 'Isn't she beautiful?' and 'I love her outfit' or 'That looks delicious', even when the woman is only drinking a coffee.

"You're really into France, huh?" Alice says.

Minnie suddenly looks a bit shy. "Um, it's a new thing. But, yeah." Her eyes dart quickly to her desk.

"New things are good," Alice says.

Minnie visibly relaxes. "Yeah, new things are great. But in a way, it could also be a destiny thing. I mean, I was named after a French cat."

Alice spends the rest of the night stroking Minnie's hair saying, "*Ooh la la, mon petit chat.*"

Before I leave, I spot the application for the French exchange on her desk. I spy that it's still blank.

Later that night, Alice starts a chat group for the three of us and sends us gifs of cats and photos of French things like baguettes and berets.

I send a message to say thank you for introducing me to madeleines, French movies and, most importantly, for the dress, which I'm really excited to wear.

Minnie replies instantly. 'You're so welcome!' – and then sends a cat emoji.

I send one back of a croissant and then I send her a separate message, privately.

"You need to fill in that form."

She doesn't reply.

ALICE

The ball is tomorrow night and I've had it in my mind I'm going to complete week eight of the programme before it. Which means squeezing in a twenty-eight-minute run tonight. I'm just getting ready to go when that annoying pest, my favourite aunt, Juliet makes a surprise appearance.

"Hello, beautiful," she says, as I open the door. Fudge.

"Wow, Juliet, what a nice surprise!"

"I knew I would be!" she says, as she barges in with a bulky bag in her hand. "And, it gets better!"

"Go on . . ." Go on, Juliet, hurry up and then please kindly go on away . . .

"I've got a present for you, because I am the best aunt in the world."

"Yippee, I love presents. Is it one of those friendship cheques that says I owe you a three-hour photo session trying to take the perfect profile picture? Because you spent that in advance last weekend."

"Ha, cheeky. No, it's an actual present that you will love and really I should save it for Chrimbo cos it's so good, but I think you might need it tomorrow."

I look at the bag in her hand. It's a Tesco bag for life and is not giving me any clues.

"Is it . . . Bombay party mix?"

"No, but if you've got some of that I'll have some too, thanks."

"Geez, Juliet, can you get on with it please? I might die from suspense otherwise."

She opens the bag and I immediately spot the telltale red box.

"SQUEEEEE!" I squeal, as I dive on to her smothering

her face in kisses. "Is it what I think it is? It better be or I want these kisses back!"

Inside the box are the beautiful golden chariot trainers. In my size.

"It's too much! But thank you thank you I'm soooooo happy I loveeee them I love you but I love them more!!"

"Well, as you rightly pointed out, mine were box fresh, and I have a friend who works at the store so he agreed to exchange mine for a different size. I guess I have a lot of trainers anyway."

Oh my goodness, this is the icing on the cake to my lizard queen outfit. It's the chariots to my feet. I'm so thrilled I put them on immediately and go and put my outfit on again to show her the final look.

"Looks amaze, babe. Shall I come round tomorrow night to do your hair?"

"Yaaas, Queen!!!"

"K. Can't stop. I'm going to the gym now."

I leap up the stairs to change out of my ball outfit and put my running gear on. I am going to fly tonight, I just know it. I swap my gorgeous goldies for Mum's yucky basics. She has seen me in these several times now so I think we've both agreed that if I don't point out that she hasn't been to Zumba in three months, I can keep her trainers.

I switch Sarah on before I even leave the house, then I burst out of the front door and straight into a light jog.

I'm smiling into the cool night air, thinking about how brilliant I'm going to look tomorrow night and how everything is coming up Alice! I'm smiling as I run past a familiar car, and a very confused Aunt Juliet looks up at me from the driver's seat.

She hasn't gone yet.

Flapjacks.

What do I do? Keep running? Or go back and explain myself? Mum and Dad know anyway. Maybe they've already told her. I decide to do a Dory and just keep swimming. Running. I just keep running.

I run for twenty-eight minutes non-stop and when Sarah counts down the final ten seconds, I run a little bit faster because I can. No one lurks in the bushes taking photos of me. Last night's run is banished to dust. The night air is cool and crisp. I feel tired and happy and warm and achey and I love it. I've completed week eight, and tomorrow night, I get to celebrate!

PART FIVE: FLYING

MINNIE

Daniel will be here to pick me up for the ball in five minutes and I'm suddenly feeling unsure about my outfit. It's very different for me. A totally new look, in fact. And now I've done it, I'm nervous. What if everyone laughs at me?

I think about that girl Aimee that Lena told me about. She might laugh. But Captain Bella and Sophie won't. Lena Singleton won't. Alice Daly-Donne won't. And Daniel won't. And really, what does one Aimee matter to me?

The doorbell goes. My stomach drops. Oh god, what if he laughs?

"I'm coming!" I yelp. I give myself one final look over in the mirror. Starting with my pointy patent stilettos. They're sugar pink and just peeping out from my black wide-legged trousers, dark and heavy with a satin side stripe, perfectly matching the collar and buttons on my cropped tuxedo jacket, fastened over a pale pink camisole. My hair is pulled back into my usual ponytail but I've added a quiff at the front, and I've followed a make-up tutorial online for a pretty pink blush and a powdery pink eyeshadow with thick full lashes and a dark berry stained lip. I've even run some dark powder through my eyebrows, just like the video said to.

I step back and think this might be the best I've ever looked. But it will only work if I wear it with confidence. I hold my head high and shout, "Are you ready for this?" and I hear his voice, honest and earnest.

"I can't wait any longer!"

I step out into the hallway and carefully descend the stairs, careful not to trip on my wide trousers.

Daniel's mouth actually hangs open. He takes it all in, up and down, and when I'm just a few steps from the bottom he breaks into his biggest smile. It's my favourite face in all the world.

"Wow," he says finally. He's running his hands up and down my arms, like he's keeping me warm. Like I've finished a race and he's proud of me. "Just . . . wow!"

I think about the application form for Paris. I've started filling it in. It feels like betrayal.

LENA

Alice's mum comes to pick me up. Jacob Porter is already in the front so I squeeze in the back between Alice and her little sister Clara, strapped into her car seat.

"Wow, Alice, your friend's outfit is much nicer than yours."

"Lena, this is Clara. Clara, don't talk to Lena."

"Did you see her shoes? They're like princess shoes – all silvery! Much better for a ball than trainers."

"Quiet time, Clara!"

The ball is being held at the school. Only the sixth form leavers' ball gets held at a swanky hotel, but the school hall looks nice all done up and there's a proper band playing. Alice looks awesome in her green jumpsuit and gold trainers. Jacob Porter is wearing a dark suit with embroidered flowers on it. He really suits it. I feel really good in Minnie's dress and even the shoes feel comfortable . . . so far.

We head into the hall and someone calls my name.

"Hey, Lena, aren't you even going to say hi?"

"I'll catch you up," I say to Alice and Jacob, and turn to face them.

Aimee looks like a doll. Giant hair, giant eyes, tiny dress, tiny body. Tasha and Nikki are dressed in slightly bulkier, darker versions of Aimee's dress, which is made of tiny golden sequins. They look like they're in mourning. Maybe they're grieving their own personalities. Aimee looks like a glass of champagne next to them. All fun times and bubbles. How did she convince them to dress as her backdrop? I don't even want to know.

"You look like you're wearing someone else's clothes," Aimee says. Not an insult. Just a fact. A true fact. So why does it cut like a surgeon's scalpel? Straight to the heart of the matter.

"I am. I borrowed it . . . from a friend."

"Looks amazing," Nikki whispers. Aimee silences her with an eyebrow.

"Thanks, Nikki."

"So, you and Big Alice and Gay Jacob are best friends now?"

Before I can answer, Seb and the boys come in. Aimee flicks her hair around and squeezes forward. Positioning herself next to me, like we're friends again.

"Hi Seb, nice suit!" she says. "Come on, let's dance!" And she grabs my hand and drags me to the dance floor. Someone else grabs my other hand and I look back to see Seb's cheeky grin. The others duly follow.

Tasha giggles next to Max. Nikki seems to get pushed out of the circle as we dance and Aimee is laughing at nothing as she bumps into Seb. He doesn't even notice her as his eyes search me out and when I glance at him, he steps forward into my space.

"Hi, Lena. You look so good."

"Thanks. You look nice in your suit."

"Only nice?" I don't know what else to say. "Can we dance later, just the two of us?" He tries to find my hand again.

He's shouting over the music and I look up to see that Aimee has heard every word.

I slip my hand away. "It's a party, Seb. Not *Strictly*!"

He laughs. "You'd get a ten from me!"

"Oh my goodness, looks like Nikki gets a ten from Lewis!" We look over and they're dancing together, hips and lips almost connected.

"Ah yeah, he's liked her for ages. Good for him." Then he shouts over to them. "Too spicy for school, guys!" but they don't break away. I look around for Aimee. Here, proof that Lewis never liked me and the smug satisfaction that the only one of us getting a snog tonight is Nikki! But she's nowhere to be seen.

ALICE

Lena's dragged away by some boys before I can introduce her to Jodie and Caro and then I'm dragged away by Jacob Porter before I can be introduced to Swedish Ant and Dec. Jacob says the best parties always happen in the kitchens. But we're at school so the closest we can get is the canteen, which has been balled-up too, with white tablecloths and some big bows around the chairs like it's a wedding. Sweet, really. There are little canapés and plastic champagne flutes filled with lemonade. We are toasting with our fourth glass in about four minutes and I'm wondering how long I can put off going for a wee when Jacob grabs my hand and says, "Let's go and drink the next glass in front of the art displays like we're at a city gallery opening." Sounds reasonable to me.

An exhibition of student art has been put on display around the other sports hall. There's no music in there, no canapés and therefore no other people. Jacob wanders around making up arty commentaries on the use of colour.

"Mmm, this one really speaks to me, darling."

I go with his flow. "Me too, darling, I really love the way the artist has chosen to put some paint on some paper. So evocative!"

"Mmm, and that choice of paper. A little provocative don't you think? A3, surely the most risqué of all the papers?" He waggles his eyebrows suggestively.

"And that passionate use of Crayola pencil crayon. So moving!" I mime-dab my overcome eyes.

"This one is really good." Jacob forgets his 'darling' voice.

"Darling, they're all good. It's an art show. They're in frames and that's how we *know* they're good."

"No, but Alice, this one is *really* good." He's serious now, so I walk over to the one he's looking at.

Bloody hell. I take a few steps back to take it all in. Furious pencil shadings in a rainbow of greys. Dark shadows and bright highlights. A dusky night scene. Three girls; powerful, focused, strong and beautiful. Two fluid figures flank a defined central girl, her face brought into focus as she charges forward. She's determined; a runner on a mission. A runner who looks just like me.

I look at the label.

'Runners, by Jacob Altman.'

"That one," I'm almost panting, "is definitely my favourite."

MINNIE

There's a little photo booth thing set up in the entrance hall and we pose for some silly photos at the ball. I can't relax properly and my 'silly face' just looks like I'm scared. Everyone is looking at me in my tuxedo but I can't really tell if they like what they see. I feel sick, and I can't tell if it's the outfit or my maybe-secret-plan-to-go-to-Paris-for-summer.

Daniel keeps spinning me out to look at me again and telling me how cool I look tonight – how pretty I am.

"So chic!" he says. "So French!"

"Why do you say that?" I feel found out.

"That's what you're into at the moment? Isn't it? It's cool! I like it. Didn't the French invent kissing?" He pulls me in close and looks deep into my eyes. "It's very difficult for me to not mess up your new lipstick. But trust me, I really want to."

And because I love him, I just ask him, straight out. "Do you think I should apply for the Summer Programme in Paris?"

". . . Not what I thought you were going to say, but yeah, sure, why not?"

Why not.

"Because I'd be gone?"

"Yeah, but only for a month."

"Is that OK?"

He laughs. "I think I can cope for four weeks, Min. So long as you FaceTime me and speak sexy French things to me and then you come back and show me some French kissing."

I wrap my arms around him and squeeze him tight. Why did I ever think he would be anything other than Daniel-like about this?

Captain Bella clears her throat in the microphone and then shouts, "Shut up, everyone, it's my time to talk!"

She gives me a little wave from her podium. She's in charge of the student awards tonight so she's up on the stage announcing them. They're mostly academic prizes – top student in maths, winner of the art prize for our year group, etc. But there are some silly categories too – Epic Fail of the Year, Selfie Queen and Selfie King. Daniel wins a science prize and he goes up to the stage waving and smiling at everyone. He gets a big cheer.

Captain Bella grabs the mic again and says, "While you're up here, Dan, we might as well bring your lady up too because Minnie and Daniel have been named Couple of the Year!"

Daniel leans into the mic and yells, "Sometimes the nerd gets the girl!" and everyone laughs.

I make my way up the steps to the stage and Bella says, "Can I also just say that Minnie should win best dressed because she looks absolutely stunning tonight!" and actually, everyone claps and cheers like they agree. I know they can't *all* agree, and I don't look into the crowd to see who isn't clapping, but I can hear a general consensus and that's enough for me. Daniel scoops me into a hug and says, "Hell, yeah!" We leave the stage holding hands and clap the rest of the prize-winners.

Bella wins 'Sportsperson of the Year' and she has to award it to herself. She says, "I want to thank Minnie Michaels for taking some time off this year to let someone else win this award."

LENA

I find Aimee in a toilet cubicle. Crying. Up close, her false eyelashes look like caterpillars. Her tears are leaving streaks through her foundation. I hand her a tissue and she dabs carefully around her eyeliner.

"I'm not crying about Seb. I'm not even bothered if you like him."

"OK."

"Do you like him?"

"Not like that, I don't think."

"Well, you can."

"I know."

She stops and looks at me, briefly outraged that I would be so bold, before she sinks back into her sniffle.

We hear a big cheer coming from the main hall. They're doing the student awards.

We hear Daniel Turner's name being called out over the PA.

"Oh god, he would win something, wouldn't he?"

"What's your problem with Daniel Turner?"

"He's just fake."

"What? How do you mean?"

"He was into me before he liked Minnie."

"Oh. OK?"

"When he joined our school, I got seated next to him in Biology before anyone realised he's a massive geek and he got moved up to top sets of everything. Anyway, in those lessons he was really into me – asking me loads of questions about the school and everything – I helped him loads and he was so nice and funny and then I hear he's suddenly in love with Minnie Michaels, but I liked him first—" she stops herself with a little gasp.

Like she didn't mean to say that at the end. "So, he lead me on, don't you think?"

"Oh, um, well, I'm not sure. Did he ever ask you out or say he liked you?"

"Well, no, it was obvious though. Both times he sat right next to me out of choice."

"So, it was just two lessons you had together?"

"Well, yeah . . . but we talked the whole time. Like two whole hours. Twice. They were double lessons."

I have no idea how to break this to her. How can she have been stewing on this for that long?

"Aimee, I . . . I don't think you can be mad about this."

The space between us hangs in the air. It's a new space where I'm straight with her and she doesn't know where she fits. I can see the two options above her head. Open up, be real and try to move on. Be a better person. Or shut it out. Block it off. Keep your head down and just smash into the world like a fist.

She isn't ready to make the change yet.

"I'm not even mad about it. Don't be stupid. I just think he's fake. Seb is fake too. Boys only want one thing. I'm not even interested in those idiots. I'm going to my cousin's house after here, she's going to sneak me into a club."

"OK, Aimee." We exit the toilets together but I know

this is where we're going to split for good. I think of the photo of us that I've got at home. Two little girls, smothered in face paints, smiles that can't be faked. It's just not who we are any more.

Minnie and Daniel are standing to the side of the stage. Minnie looks amazing in a tuxedo suit. She's smiling and clapping for her netball captain.

Aimee spots her. "Oh my god, what is she wearing? She doesn't have a clue. Clinging to him because she hasn't got any real friends. Isn't she pathetic?" One last desperate attempt to find something we can bitch about.

"Hey, Minnie! Over here!" I am already gone.

ALICE

I'm running. I have to find Other Jacob. I glide past Jodie and Kevin and Caro and Marcus; I can't tell who is wrapped around who. I'm zooming in and out of the crowd. So glad I'm wearing my trainers. Jacob Porter has gone on stage to accept his 'Social of the Year' award. Apparently, he does these hilarious live posts from registration every morning and his form tutor has no idea. I really should pay more attention online. Why are all these boys wearing the same-coloured suits? How am I meant to find Snow White in a sea of black jackets? His hair is camouflaged in formal wear. I jog all around the main hall and back through the canteen. I lurk around the toilets and check every bin in the building – we all know what good hook-up places they are. No Jacob. Has he even come to the ball?

I'm about to check his socials – when I see a lone figure in the other hall. Of course Other Jacob would be in the other hall. He's there, by his drawing. I walk in and I'm trying to decide whether to go with something flirty like, 'Did someone order a Muse?' or just be straightforward and say, 'Look, Other Jacob, do you fancy me or what?' but he surprises me by talking first.

"So, do you like it? Are you mad with me?"

What? Mad with you? Are you kidding? I am madly in danger of trying to kiss you.

"No! Yes! Yes, to the first bit. I love it and no, I'm not mad at you. I love it!"

Smooth. Did someone order a Muse?

He smiles. Bashful and Happy. Let's not get into the seven dwarves thing again.

"I wasn't spying on you, the first time. I was trying to take a picture of the houses in the dark, some of them have the weird gargoyle things on their gates, I thought I could draw them. But then I saw you."

"Alternative gargoyle."

He laughs. "Not what I meant."

"So, you took my picture instead."

"The funny thing was, my photo didn't even work. It was too dark. And you don't wear anything reflective, which is really dangerous in the dark by the way."

"Noted, thank you."

"So, when I realised it was a regular thing, I thought I'd try again and get a new picture, or maybe we'd just stop and chat or something. I don't know. I didn't mean to turn it into a thing where I was actually hiding in the bushes waiting for you."

"Oh, well, these things happen."

"And I thought I'd add in your friends. Do you really like the picture?"

"Yes, because you made me look amazing and like a proper runner who goes out running all the time."

"Well, you are?"

"Amazing looking? Thanks. No, I meant a proper runner."

"You are a runner." He takes a step towards me. "And you always look amazing."

"No, like a proper one though."

"Why do you keep saying that? You are a proper

runner." Another few steps towards me.

"But I'm just practising. I'm not doing it for real yet."

"But I've seen you out running loads of times." He takes my hand. Bit brazen for Snow White.

"Eh?"

He slips his arm around my waist. He's laughing gently. "I don't understand. You're running in public. In our town, near our school, near my house. I've seen you running several times a week for the past two months."

"Geez Louise, Jacob, where on earth do you live?!" God, he is gorgeous.

He pulls me close. For an accidental stalker, he's overcoming his shyness pretty rapidly "By the hospital. On the road before the alley."

"SCRUPLES?" Our noses are touching.

"No, next door. Anyway, can I kiss you now?"

"Oh, yes please."

MINNIE

I spend the next two hours dancing with Daniel, Lena, Alice and two guys named Jacob. One of them seems to be Alice's boyfriend and the other one is like Alice's girlfriend. They're all lovely. We all sing at the top of our voices and take turns dancing through a tunnel of arms.

I slow dance with Daniel and then we all swap partners and I silly slow dance with Lena and Alice and we are laughing like we're the oldest friends. I think that in the future we will be. When they play 'Bohemian Rhapsody' everyone does this really over the top headbanging and my bobble just spontaneously combusts. My hair is all over the place, I didn't realise quite how long it was. "I'm trying to get Alice to join our running club," Lena says to me as Alice takes it upon herself to comb my hair through with her fingers and fix my quiff.

"You. Look. Awesome," she tells me.

In the toilets, I look at myself in the mirror. I do look kind of awesome. Two girls from my English class say it too as I'm refreshing my lipstain.

"I wish I could pull something like that off," one says, eyeing up my tux.

"I love that lip colour on you!" says the other. I think I might get my hair cut this weekend. I'm enjoying this new look thing.

I come out of the toilets and bump straight into Aimee, who spills her drink on my shoes and laughs.

"Wrong toilet. Suits go in there." She points to the

Men's. Her gang of followers, all dressed in black, giggle like little witches trick or treating.

"Ha, yeah, OK," I say, because I don't know if she's joking.

"So, are you ditching your Aussie for Lena Singleton and Big Alice now?" She looks to her friends for another laugh.

"What? No."

"Isn't this your coming-out outfit?"

"What are you talking about?"

"Oh, come on, everyone knows Lena is as gay as her dad." Her gaggle gasp.

"Huh? What has that got to do with anything?" I ask. I am bewildered by this person.

"And, to be fair, I might not be." Lena stands in front of me.

"Whatever, Lena, we all know it's coming."

Alice jumps in out of nowhere. "What's coming?"

Aimee not-so-subtly points at Alice's trainers and turns to roll her eyes at her friends.

"DO YOU LIKE THEM?" Alice shouts, as if Aimee is hard of hearing.

"What?" Aimee looks offended to even be addressed by Alice.

"MY TRAINERS. DO YOU LIKE THEM? ARE YOUR

SHOES HURTING? DO YOU WANT TO BORROW MINE FOR A BIT?"

Aimee looks mortified. "What? No! Stop shouting, you idiot. I don't want your skanky shoes." Other people around us turn to look at what is going on.

"WAS THERE SOMETHING ELSE YOU WANTED THEN?"

"No. Go away, Alice. I am allowed to talk to Lena if I want to."

"OH, RIGHT LET ME JUST CHECK." Alice turns to Lena, who is shaking with laughter. "LENA. DO YOU WANT TO TALK TO THIS GIRL?"

Lena's laughter erupts. "NO THANKS," she shouts back.

"OK, WE'RE GOING TO HANG UP NOW. BYE, THANKS, DON'T @ ME." Alice wraps one arm around Lena's neck and the other around my waist and off we go.

"You should really come running with us," I say to Alice when we're back on the dancefloor.

Alice is looking past me, beaming at the dark-haired Jacob who looks smitten. "Yeah, maybe I will," she calls behind her as she dances towards him.

BE
MORE

PART SIX: WINNING

ALICE

I've been out twice this week for my run and both times I haven't even made it to 'Scruples'. Jacob's house is just before it, and on both occasions he's just happened to be in his garden as I've been power-walking past. This is not because he is a keen gardener and, OK, I might have told him I was going to be going past in the next few minutes by texting him before I left, but it's super cute how he's waiting for me with a little drink and a snack.

"Come in for five minutes?" he says. And I stay an hour chatting to his mum in the kitchen. He shows me some of the practise sketches for his piece. He looks shy when he sees me notice the school bookmark pinned to his easel, Alice side up. We haven't kissed again since the ball but there seems to be an understanding that we're sort of together now. I feel the kiss brewing though. I think it's going to be even better than the first time.

I'm not going to text him tonight; I really need to complete this run.

I'm going out FOR A RUN I type out. And then I delete it and lace up my trainers.

I walk quickly to warm up.

This is my penultimate run. Not that my first one this week should really count but I'm running out of days and I need to finish this within the nine weeks so it's this one tonight and then my final, final, FINAL tomorrow.

No rest day. No time. I know I am the captain of my own soul and master of my own fate and that it is completely possible for me to take another day to complete the app, but I did not sign up to learn to run for thirty minutes in 'nine weeks and one day'. That is the worst name for an app ever. No one would download that.

Enough stalling brain, let's run.

And I do. But it's hard. Like really hard. Harder than last week, even though we haven't got to the final additional two minutes yet. We're only at minute fourteen and I want to die. I want to give up, so I can die more comfortably.

This is torture. Everything hurts and I just want to stop. I start to panic and my breathing loses its rhythm. I'm doing short sharp breaths that aren't helping me at all and I start to splutter and choke. My feet speed up, as if I can outrun this disaster. Get away from it quicker. Maybe up ahead I'm doing well in minutes seventeen and eighteen. I drop back, trying to find my pace again. I'm confused. I'm a mess. I knew I wasn't a runner.

I stop.

I've failed.

Shut up. Go away.

I don't want to talk about it.

Alice Daly-Donne is typing . . .

LENA

Alice texts our group about her horrible run. We tell her again that it's totally normal. That Usain Bolt has bad days. That sometimes you really are just tired, or not in the zone. The zone really exists. And that it doesn't mean you won't ever be in the zone again. You could be in the zone again by tomorrow. You could even be in the zone an hour later.

I will be in bed in an hour. With a book and a slice of Battenberg, **she replies.**

Fair enough. That sounds good too, **I reply.** I think Alice just needs some time to cool off tonight.

I scroll back up our chat to look at the screenshot she sent us after the ball. It's a photo of a drawing Jacob Altman did of the three of us running. Minnie and I are just vague shapes really, but you can tell it's us by our hair. I think he copied us from one of the bookmarks but it isn't really a picture of us at all. It's of Alice. She looks incredible. Fierce and beautiful and so strong. Jacob really sees her. And he must *really* like her. It's right there in his drawing; all of his feelings. I just hope Alice can see herself like this. I send the picture back to her again, just as a reminder. This is you.

I message Minnie privately and we make a plan to miss our next running club. We need to make that drawing a reality.

Minnie is totally on board with my plan, but she clearly has a plan of her own too.

Daniel wanted to know if you want to come out for burgers this weekend with us . . . and Sebastian Edwards.

Ha! Whose idea was that?

Seb's, I think!

I try and picture Seb's face. I think about his lips and whether I might be interested in kissing them. I have no idea. I guess I wouldn't know until it was about to happen. I think about how he makes me laugh. And how much I like talking to him. And how much I like eating burgers. And then I think why should it be any more complicated than that?

OK. Sounds like fun. But if I do this, you have to promise me you'll complete that application form.

Deal.

MINNIE

I'm doing it. I'm in the chair with the towels tucked around my neck and the black cape on. I'm sipping a cappuccino with my wet hair all combed out around me. The application form is in my bag at my feet. I have filled it in, like I promised Lena. I've even had it signed by my teachers. I just haven't been able to post it yet.

"Are you sure?" my stylist, Rani, asks me one last time.

"I am!"

And she snips a huge chunk out of my hair. Quickly followed by four more large cuts to take the majority off the length. I decide not to look in the mirror until she's done and focus on my coffee and my magazine. I feel the scissors snipping furiously around my ears and every now and then a little wet ribbon of hair lands on my lap. The hairdryer comes out and there's some tugging with a brush, then some more snipping and flicking and I'm desperate to peek at what's going on.

The magazine has an article about trying out olive and khaki as eyeshadows and I make a mental note of a metallic eyeliner in goldy green that looks really pretty.

"Take a look!" Rani says, when I've actually forgotten what's going on.

And I look up, through my new chunky blunt fringe. I run my fingers through my new tousled bob, feeling the air when I run out of hair. I shake my head in the mirror, to check it's really me. I look totally different. But like someone I might notice on the street. Someone who looks sort of effortlessly cool. Dare I say it, someone . . . chic?

LENA

I'm eating a banana before I go and get Minnie. Dad comes in and steals a bite.

He puts his phone down on the counter. An alert lights up the screen just long enough for me to see the photograph he has set as his wallpaper. It's me, just the other night, all dressed up ready for the ball. He made me pose awkwardly by the foot of the stairs. I felt so shy and embarrassed.

"Dad, why have you got that awful picture on your phone!"

"Don't you say that about my new favourite photo!" He picks up the phone and lights up the screen again to look at it. "I've shown it to everyone. I say, 'Look at my girl. Look at my beautiful grown-up girl!'"

"Dad, that is SO embarrassing!"

"Don't ever be embarrassed to be yourself, Lena. This one is going on THE WALL."

The wall is a space where Dad started sticking photos of me when I was little. Now they're all overlapped and haphazard, crowding my official adoption certificate that is framed in the middle. He used to not let any of the pictures touch the frame. I guess the memories of our life together are more important to him than the legal stuff now because they have taken over everything. Little Lena learns to walk with a toy dog on wheels. Lena wears a giant hat. Lena with chocolate round her mouth. Lena's tenth birthday. Lena with Henry. Lena with her old best friend, Aimee, covered in face paints. Lena on holiday writing her name in the sand.

Lena starting secondary school. Now Lena's summer ball. Lena Lena Lena . . .

I look at the photos now and realise something I have never noticed before; not one of them is Lena running.

". . . Are these really your favourite memories of me?"

"Some of them." He comes and stands next to me. "The ones I have photos of. Sometimes, I'm enjoying myself too much to remember to get the camera out."

"Like when I race?" Would there be a photo if I was a winner?

"I love to see you run! I'm so happy you've joined my club. We can add a photo of you running, if you like."

"You've been to loads of my races – why isn't there a picture? Isn't that our thing? Don't you want me to be a winner?"

He stops and looks at me like he's realising something too.

"I will support you in anything, Lena. If that's racing—"

"No," I cut in. "It isn't." The truth cracks the air like a starting pistol. And just like that, I know – he never thought it was. He thought that was *my* thing and he went with it. Those early mornings. Those late nights. Always just to be with me.

"My girl, our thing is anything we do together. Laughing is our thing. Pancakes is our thing." He draws me into a quick daddy-bear hug. "Shall I make some batter now?"

"I'm going to help some friends tonight," I say. "But actually, there is a photo I'd like to add to the wall." I rummage in my school bag and give him one of the prints I secretly bought. Minnie, Alice and me; sitting together laughing about nothing on a cold bench outside the school library. It was really hard to muster up any smiles that day. It felt so staged. Minnie was so try-hard and I wasn't trying at all. Alice was just Alice but I didn't know that yet. She kept trying to get us to say silly things when the camera was going and I was having none of it because I was horrible, but Minnie tried her best to join in. When the photographer was fiddling with some more settings Alice said something like, "When he next does his countdown, let's all burst into song." Minnie sounded unsure, but she asked what song. "Twinkle, Twinkle, Little Star," Alice had said, "that will really creep him out."

So, the photographer had come back over and prepared us for another shot. "Ready, girls, 3-2-1."

"TWIIIIIINKLE." For some reason, Minnie really went

for it. Alice hadn't really sung and obviously I was never going to, but Minnie had just gone for it. In this high-pitched choirgirl voice. Totally seriously. And Alice absolutely collapsed with laughter and it got me. I laughed. And then Minnie realised what had happened and she started giggling. The photographer took that shot.

"Are these the friends you're going to meet?" Dad asks.

"Yep. Alice and Minnie . . . We're going for a run."

"They could come for pancakes too?" I see that happening in the future. Definitely. Minnie would love Dad's pancakes and Alice would make him laugh. I am already looking forward to it.

"Another time, Dad, but we have to do this now. But I'll be back for dinner."

"Got it. In that case, Lena. Is it OK if I invite someone to join us? Someone I'd like you to meet?"

My heart flutters on my dad's behalf. Yes! "Yes! I'd really love that." If he's worth my dad's saltfish and ackee, I can't wait to meet him – and then I add, "Coach . . . you're a good dad," and I wonder if I've ever said that before. "Want to do a selfie before I go?" He leaps up and pulls me close and we squash into the frame. I smile with my whole soul. Even though there's no reason why we should, I always thought we kind of looked alike.

"That's another one for THE WALL," he shouts as I let the door close behind me.

ALICE

OK, so I had a bad run yesterday but I need to get past it. I try to remember what Lena and Minnie's messages said. Something about the Twilight Zone and how today I'm in a different zone and that's the zone where I can totally do this. I think about Jacob's drawing.

I send a message to my running girls. I'm positive. I'm confident.

Congratulate me in half an hour. I'm going to do this.

I hear epic music in my mind as I lace up my trainers. Mum's trainers. I still don't wear my chariots for running. I feel like I walk down the hall in slow motion, like astronauts walking towards their final mission. Obviously, I'm in less danger of getting lost in space or blowing up. But there is that spontaneous human combustion thing to think about and I do get pretty hot when I'm running. I look out the window to see if Philip wants to come with me, as if he could know the significance of this session to complete our journey, but he's wrestling with a tea towel and looks pretty into it.

I should probably do this on my own . . .

I open the front door and I'm hit with a sudden punch of nerves. My stomach drops and momentarily I can't imagine completing a thirty-minute run. It seems impossible. Huge. Agonising. And lonely.

I turn out of my gate and, amazingly, ridiculously, there are my friends in real life – Lena Singleton and Minnie Michaels, and my boy, Other Jacob. For some inexplicable reason, Lena has written 'BE MORE ALICE' on a piece of paper and pinned it to her t-shirt. I like it though.

"We thought you might need some support," Minnie says, shaking her freshly chopped bob in the breeze.

"Well, you'd be exactly right." I feel something cringe rise up in my throat and I say it anyway. "Actually, I want to say something cringe – Lena, you were the first person to sneak into my secret running club and you totally saved me. Minnie, and I'm sorry to bring it up again, but you looking all tragic and floppy in that ambulance really motivated me and I think about your neck whenever I run."

"That's sweet, and weird," Minnie says.

"Also, you look *très chic.*" She looks beaut.

". . . And I thought you might need this." Jacob leans in

and gives me a perfectly polite peck on the lips. It's lovely, but I can't help myself from pulling him in again.

Our lips smoosh into each other and I assume Minnie and Lena are whistling and looking at the trees because this is an embarrassing snog to be standing so close too. I run my hand through his hair and lean into his lovely warmth. He wraps his arms around me and squeezes me tightly and I think about saying, 'Forget the run, girls' but Lena interrupts me before I can pull away and says, "That's enough support from you, Jacob!" He pulls back, looking pink and shy.

I tell him that was yummy and thank you and let's pick that up again when I've finished.

"Game face on, Alice!" Lena barks, and then she turns to Minnie, "You too, Michaels, because we're running via a postbox and you are going to post that application!"

"But I haven't got it with me!" Minnie cries. *Zut alors!*

"That's because I've got it. I grabbed it from your desk when I came to pick you up."

Sacré bleu. Lena is a woman possessed.

"Have you ever thought about being a coach?" I ask her.

"Stop procrastinating! We're doing this!!!"

Blimey! Sarah never *actually* shouts at me.

"Are you ready?" Minnie says, looking deep into my eyes, searching for insecurities to squash. I grab one of her hands and say *"Oui!"*

Lena takes my other hand. She nods at me with all the confidence in the world; there is not a doubt in her mind that I can do this.

"Let's run."

And we do. We are Jacob's picture come to life. Not quite poetry in motion, something sweatier and sillier, but something that was only imagined is turned real.

As Lena announces the final thirty seconds, I feel like I'm going to explode (different to combusting). I speed up, I can't help it. I'm too excited. Lena and Minnie easily match me but I keep going faster and faster. I know I shouldn't risk another sudden stop like this but I just can't stop. They catch me and Lena shouts, "TEN SECONDS TO GO."

"YOU. ARE. RUNNING!" Minnie howls into the sky. Three girls roar in reply, our hot breath making plumes of smoke rise up. We are fiery little dragons. We are fierce. We are friends. "WE. ARE. RUNNING!" And then it's just

5

4

3

2

1

WWWAARRRRGHHHHHHHHHHHHHHH!!!!!

Lena and Minnie leap on me and we hold hands and jump around in a circle like children in a playground squealing and giggling into the air.

I get my phone out of my pocket to take a picture and find the final running track has been playing in my pocket this whole time. I play the final few minutes out loud. It's Sarah saying well done. She says how brilliantly I've done over the programme. How committed I've been and how the results speak for themselves – proof that I've put the hard work in. I feel a bit emosh. Sarah says this is just the start of my running journey, really. From here I've got the tools to progress, and I can always download the 10K app if I want. (Calm down, Sarah.) Lena says, "Heck yes!" Maybe it isn't impossible to imagine, but I don't think I'll need Sarah again. I think about running with Lena and Minnie; the light-footed friends who found me in the dark. Maybe I'll even go to that club with them. I think about Jacob, waiting for me when I come back, with a hot chocolate and little cuddle. I think about going to the gym with Juliet, and surprising her on the treadmill. We never really did discuss it when she saw me heading out. I think about being an old lady. Running in my sixties, which I can, because I've done it since I was a teenager.

This feels like groundwork. This is who I am now. I run. I'm a runner.

MINNIE

We do our cool-down walk to the nearest postbox in silence. Breathing hard and smiling hard and squeezing each other's arms. Alice is victorious. She has finished her challenge. Mine is only just beginning, but she's inspiring. They both are. I'm going to do this.

Lena takes the envelope from her pocket and hands it to me. For some reason all three of us hold the envelope as I push it through the slot. I feel it immediately. Weightlessness. Happiness. Relief. Joy. Excitement. Everything that's to come. *Allons-y!*

I let out a sigh and Alice says, "Minnie, even your sighs are starting to sound French," and then we're laughing like maniacs again. "Maybe we will all apply for the Paris Marathon?" I'm being silly, but as I say it, I imagine future Minnie doing it.

Lena says she'd like to do a marathon one day too. Alice tells us to calm down and suggests a movie marathon and Lena says her dad still calls Snickers bars 'Marathons' so I think we agree that at some point before I go to Paris, we'll all watch a ton of DVDs and eat chocolate.

Our soft trainers barely make a sound as we meander home, as if we're treading lightly on our new ground together, though it already feels so solid.

We come to the split in the road. Alice is going left to Jacob's house and Lena is going right. I'm going straight on to Daniel's house. I can't wait to tell him about this. About the run and posting the application and laughing with my friends.

We have one more massive cuddle and then Lena produces three little chocolates from her pockets and we laugh and laugh and laugh some more. Alice snaps a group selfie. To the untrained eye it appears just like those school photos, the same three girls, but it's not the same at all. We look each other in the eyes when we laugh now. Three friends. If you know, you know.

THE END

HAVE YOU EVER WONDERED HOW BOOKS ARE MADE?

UCLan Publishing is an award winning independent publisher specialising in Children's and Young Adult books. Based at The University of Central Lancashire, this Preston-based publisher teaches MA Publishing students how to become industry professionals using the content and resources from its business; students are included at every stage of the publishing process and credited for the work that they contribute.

The business doesn't just help publishing students though. UCLan Publishing has supported the employability and real-life work skills for the University's Illustration, Acting, Translation, Animation, Photography, Film & TV students and many more. This is the beauty of books and stories; they fuel many other creative industries! The MA Publishing students are able to get involved from day one with the business and they acquire a behind the scenes experience of what it is like to work for a such a reputable independent.

The MA course was awarded a Times Higher Award (2018) for Innovation in the Arts and the business, UCLan Publishing, was awarded Best Newcomer at the Independent Publishing Guild (2019) for the ethos of teaching publishing using a commercial publishing house. As the business continues to grow, so too does the student experience upon entering this dynamic Masters course.

www.uclanpublishing.com
www.uclanpublishing.com/courses/
uclanpublishing@uclan.ac.uk